One Hot FAVOR

Other Books by Anna Durand

One Hot Chance (Hot Brits, Book One)
One Hot Roomie (Hot Brits, Book Two)
One Hot Crush (Hot Brits, Book Three)
The Dixon Brothers Trilogy (Hot Brits, Books 1-3)
One Hot Escape (Hot Brits, Book Four)
One Hot Rumor (Hot Brits, Book Five)
One Hot Christmas (Hot Brits, Book Six)
One Hot Scandal (Hot Brits, Book Eight)
One Hot Bash (Hot Brits, Book Ten)
Natural Obsession (Au Naturel Nights, Book One)
Natural Deception (Au Naturel Nights, Book Two)
Natural Passion (Au Naturel Trilogy, Book One)
Natural Impulse (Au Naturel Trilogy, Book Two)
Lachlan in a Kilt (The Ballachulish Trilogy, Book One)
Aidan in a Kilt (The Ballachulish Trilogy, Book Two)
Rory in a Kilt (The Ballachulish Trilogy, Book Three)
The American Wives Club (A Hot Brits/Hot Scots/Au Naturel Crossover)
Brit vs. Scot (A Hot Brits/Hot Scots/Au Naturel Crossover)
A Novel Secret (A Hot Brits/Hot Scots/Au Naturel Crossover) (
Dangerous in a Kilt (Hot Scots, Book One)
Wicked in a Kilt (Hot Scots, Book Two)
Scandalous in a Kilt (Hot Scots, Book Three)
The MacTaggart Brothers Trilogy (Hot Scots, Books 1-3)
Gift-Wrapped in a Kilt (Hot Scots, Book Four)
Notorious in a Kilt (Hot Scots, Book Five)
Insatiable in a Kilt (Hot Scots, Book Six)
Lethal in a Kilt (Hot Scots, Book Seven)
Irresistible in a Kilt (Hot Scots, Book Eight)
Devastating in a Kilt (Hot Scots, Book Nine)
Spellbound in a Kilt (Hot Scots, Book Ten)
Relentless in a Kilt (Hot Scots, Book Eleven)
Incendiary in a Kilt (Hot Scots, Book Twelve)
Wild in a Kilt (Hot Scots, Book Thirteen)
Unstoppable in a Kilt (Hot Scots, Book Fourteen)
The Notorious Dr. MacT (A Hot Scots Prequel)
The British Bastard (A Hot Scots Prequel)
Natural Satisfaction (Au Naturel Trilogy, Book Three)
Echo Power (Echo Power Trilogy, Book One)
Echo Dominion (Echo Power Trilogy, Book Two)
Echo Unbound (Echo Power Trilogy, Book Three)
The Mortal Falls (Undercover Elementals, Book One)
The Mortal Fires (Undercover Elementals, Book Two)
The Mortal Tempest (Undercover Elementals, Book Three)
The Janusite Trilogy (Undercover Elementals, Books 1-3)
Obsidian Hunger (Undercover Elementals, Book Four)
Unbidden Hunger (Undercover Elementals, Book Five)
The Thirteenth Fae (Undercover Elementals, Book Six)
Cyneric (Undercover Elementals, Book 7)

One Hot FAVOR

Hot Brits, Book Nine

ANNA DURAND

JACORSVILLE BOOKS · MARIETTA, OHIO`

ONE HOT FAVOR

ISBN: 978-1-958144-11-4 (paperback)
ISBN: 978-1-958144-12-1 (ebook)
ISBN: 978-1-958144-13-8 (audiobook)

Manufactured in the United States.

Jacobsville Books
www.JacobsvilleBooks.com

Publisher's Cataloging-in-Publication Data
provided by Five Rainbows Cataloging Services

Names: Durand, Anna.
Title: One hot favor / Anna Durand.
Description: Marietta, OH : Jacobsville Books, 2023. | Series: Hot Brits, bk. 9.
Identifiers: ISBN 978-1-958144-11-4 (paperback) | ISBN 978-1-958144-12-1 (ebook) | ISBN 978-1-958144-13-8 (audiobook)
Subjects: LCSH: Man-woman relationships--Fiction. | Cricket--Fiction. | Sportsmanship--Fiction. | Photographers--Fiction. | British--Fiction. | Americans--Fiction. | Romance fiction. | BISAC: FICTION / Romance / Contemporary. | FICTION / Romance / Romantic Comedy. | FICTION / Romance / Sports | GSAFD: Love stories.
Classification: LCC PS3604.U724 O5442 2023 (print) | LCC PS3604.U724 (ebook) | DDC 813/.6--dc23.

Chapter One

Dominic

When the Viscount Sommerleigh demands that I visit him in his office, it means one of two things—Hugh wants to murder me, or he and his wife are plotting something. Neither option appeals to me, but I think I'd choose murder over meddling. I've known Hugh Parrish for years. But he didn't become a meddler until he married Avery, a charming American woman. Now, he and all our married mates think I need to "settle down" and "find the right woman."

Maybe I would like to do that, but not because Lord Sommerleigh commanded it. Why, then, am I striding through the halls of Sommerleigh Sweets' corporate headquarters to meet with the CEO, otherwise known as Hugh? I might be slightly curious about what he and his wife mean to do. That's all.

As I march up to the desk where Hugh's executive assistant sits, I stop to smile and greet her. "Good morning, Trudy. You look lovely today."

"Thank you, Mr. Rigby. Lord Sommerleigh is waiting for you, and he asked me to send you right in the moment you arrived."

"Can't keep the viscount waiting, can we?"

"No, sir. You can go in."

The door to Hugh's office is closed, but since I have permission, I walk right in and shut the door behind me.

Lord Sommerleigh sits behind his desk in a pose that seems too casual to be genuine. "There you are, Dom. I thought you'd forgotten about our appointment."

"How could I forget?" I drop onto a chair across the desk from him. "You texted me reminders twice a day for the past three days."

"Sorry about that. Derek thought it would be amusing to harass you with technology."

"Well, that does explain why each text also had a rude emoji attached to it."

Hugh arches his brows. "Rude emojis? You'll need to show me those."

I hold out my phone so he can see the screen.

A half-suppressed chuckle splutters out of him. "Is that a pile of shit?"

"Yes."

"Derek is American, so we must tolerate his rudeness. He can't help it."

I hook one leg over the other knee. "Are you going to tell me why you summoned me here?"

"Of course. I need your help with a project."

"Candy is your specialty, not mine. I teach schoolgirls how to play cricket."

Hugh shakes his head. "I don't want you to work for me. This project is for charity, and your skills will be essential."

"For what?"

Lord Sommerleigh steeples his fingers, eying me with a sneaky glint that I know all too well. "Avery and I are organizing a charity do. The proceeds will go to cancer research."

"What does any of that have to do with my skills?"

"Once upon a time, you were one of the top cricketers in the world. That's the skill we need." He rolls his chair up to the desk and folds his arms atop it. "We're organizing a charity cricket match with former pros competing against the current crop of players."

"I see. So, you're trying to kill me with cricket. I'm not a youngster anymore, Hugh."

He gives me an exasperated look. "Honestly, Dom, you are not an elderly gent. You're thirty-eight and still in top condition. That means for you, the charity match will be a dolly."

"An easy catch? I doubt that. And I quit cricket because of my knee."

"But it doesn't bother you anymore. I saw how you played in the casual match we held at Sommerleigh a few months ago."

My first reaction is to tell Hugh to sod off, but we've been friends for too long for me to do that. I know he means well, but honestly, I don't play anymore. If I and a gang of other former cricketers play against well-trained younger men...

We will all die.

"If a bunch of retirees compete against youngsters who train religiously, we'll need to pray for a lollipop with every bowl."

"Since when do you pray for an easy ball?" Hugh stares straight into my eyes. "Are you afraid, Dominic? The man who used to dominate the field and earned the nickname The Dom can't possibly be worried about a measly little charity match."

"Let me think about it."

"If you insist. I will need your answer by tomorrow so we can book a venue for the ball, and we'll need time to find an available cricket ground." Hugh leans back in his chair. "Perhaps the third part of the event will help you decide."

A few things he just said finally sink in. "When you say 'ball,' I assume you aren't talking about the sort cricketers use."

"No. I meant a party with dancing and music. Drinks too, naturally."

Thank heavens for that. I'll need to be quite drunk to agree to take up a bat again in a genuine match. Am I seriously considering accepting Hugh's offer? It's insane. "What is the third part of your nefarious plot?"

Hugh laughs—loudly. "Nefarious? You've become rather paranoid, haven't you?"

"Only since you invited me to your office."

The desk phone rings. Hugh snatches it up. "Yes, Trudy? Wonderful. Please do ask our guest to come in."

I squint at Hugh. "What guest?"

"You'll see."

The door swings open, and a beautiful brunette sashays into the room.

I leap out of my chair. "Chelsea? What are you doing here? You should be home in America."

"Gee, that's a great way to say hello."

"Ah, sorry. I'm surprised, that's all."

"Take a seat, Chelsea," Hugh says. "We need to inform Dominic of the plan."

I return to my chair while Chelsea takes the one beside me. Her green eyes shimmer like emeralds in the sunlight that streams through the windows.

She aims her sweet smile at me. "Hugh didn't tell you yet, did he?"

"Clearly not."

Lord Sommerleigh smirks but quickly erases that expression, replacing it with a slight smile. "We've hired Chelsea Vance Photography to take on the third project in our master plan."

I glance back and forth between Chelsea and Hugh. "Photography? Stop being so bloody coy and tell me what you're talking about."

"The calendar."

"He doesn't get it," Chelsea says. "Would you like me to explain it, Hugh?"

Lord Sommerleigh glances at his watch. "Oh, look at the time. I promised Avery I'd be home for lunch. You two should stay here and chat about the project in private. I'm sure Dom will be far more cooperative with you, Chelsea."

He practically bolts out the door.

I veer my gaze to Chelsea. "Why do I feel like I'm about to be tortured for information?"

She makes a dismissive gesture with her hand. "You're being silly. This event will be fun and painless, if you cooperate."

"Don't you have clients back home who need to have their dogs photographed? Or children who want to vomit on your shoes?"

"That rarely happens. And you're just being contrary."

I drum my fingers on my thigh. "Tell me what on earth your photographic project is all about."

"Only if you promise to genuinely consider doing it."

"Do I need to swear a blood oath? Get on with it, Chelsea."

"All right." She squares her shoulders and clears her throat. "I want you and other former pro cricketers to participate in a calendar."

"You've already mentioned that. What aren't you telling me? How will we 'participate'?"

"The calendar is aimed at adults, mostly women. But I'm sure men will buy it too, for their significant others."

Why do I feel as if she's afraid I'll fly off the handle when she tells me the whole truth? I've never done that. But Chelsea is clearly anxious.

"Let's cut to the chase," I say. "Exactly what sort of calendar will it be?"

"Beefcake."

"I don't understand."

She bites her upper lip briefly, then sucks in a deep breath. "Sexy half-naked men."

Has my jaw dropped down to my chest? No, I think it crashed to the floor. "You want me to, ah…"

I can't even finish that sentence.

Chelsea moves to crouch at my feet, resting her hands on my knees. "Please don't dismiss the idea out of hand. It's not like you've never taken your shirt off before. During Hugh and Avery's wedding week shenanigans, you had no problem with whipping your shirt off in front of everyone at the end of the cricket match."

"That was different. And the Scots instigated it, not me. I got swept along in their wake."

"You've never been shy. Why are you bent out of shape about showing a little skin for charity?"

The way she's kneeling at my feet, I have an excellent view down her blouse. Its low neckline reveals enough of her cleavage that my trousers are suddenly feeling tight in the groin. I can't help that Chelsea is sexy and that my body reacts to her sensual appeal. It does not mean I'm attracted to her. We've been mates for too long to suddenly develop lust for each other.

She pokes my chest. "Answer my question."

"What was the question again?"

Chelsea rolls her eyes. "Why are you getting weird about taking your shirt off?"

"Because you said 'half-naked.' I do not want to take my clothes off in front of you."

She studies me for a moment, and I swear I can see gears clicking away in her eyes while she figures out how to talk me into this calendar bollocks.

Then she pats my thigh and smiles. "I have an idea. Let's go to my studio and take a few test shots. That might make you more comfortable with the idea."

"I don't know."

"When I said 'half-naked,' I meant you would take your shirt off. That's all."

"Let me think about it."

"Sure. But we need your answer soon, Dominic. You can't procrastinate your way out of it."

"I won't. You have my word."

"Good." She stands up. "Now, I need to head to the studio so I can get started on the project. Other cricketers aren't as stubborn as you. They're excited to take part."

"You have a studio? Where?"

"Here in London. Hugh and Avery arranged it for me."

Of course they did. Those two need to start having babies to distract them from all this ruddy meddling.

Chelsea and I walk out of the building together, then climb into separate taxis. Will I participate in a "beefcake" calendar? I'll need to think long and hard about that.

Chapter Two

Chelsea

I snap photos in quick succession, capturing sexy images of a hot, muscular guy who isn't at all skittish about posing half-naked for a calendar. Chip Martel seems to enjoy the process, considering the way he keeps grinning and flexing his muscles. If he's trying to impress me, the tactic fails. Chip has a great body, but I don't feel any attraction for the Aussie hunk.

After one last shot, I lower my camera. "Thanks, Chip. You did great."

"Glad I could be of service." He grins again and winks. "I'll strip for you anytime."

"You can keep your pants on. This isn't a porno calendar."

He grabs his shirt and pulls it on, then winks at me. "I had a few maidens over last night, and I gave them a heavy ball."

"That's cute, but I'm friends with a cricketer. I know you're not actually talking about women. A maiden over is a cricketing term, and so is a heavy ball."

"Could I buy you a drink?"

"That's kind of you, but I have another session today." I check the time on my phone. "The next guy should be here any minute."

"Who is it? Maybe I know him."

"It's Benno Hochberg."

Chip nods with mock solemnity. "Oh, yeah, the German who defected to an English team. I guess he likes losing matches."

"But you defected to the English side."

"That's different. I'm lending them my Australian magic."

"Uh-huh." I'm not really paying attention to what he said. My focus is on prepping for the next session. "I'll let you know if I need any additional shots of you."

"Ring me anytime, Chelsea. I'm at your disposal."

Someone knocks on the door. That must be my next victim. Chip clearly doesn't feel that way about becoming a calendar star, but Dominic has been weirdly pigheaded about not wanting to take his shirt off. He seems to think I plan to drag him into a dungeon and chain him to the wall, then rip his clothes off.

That thought conjures an image in my mind of Dominic naked and restrained, at my mercy. I start to tingle down there between my thighs. I do not want to screw Dominic. I just photographed a hot guy, so naturally, I'm feeling warm and tingly. It's an autonomic response, and it will pass.

Chip swings the door open and greets Benno, who says something in what I think is German. Chip responds in the same language, and they both laugh. Benno slaps Chip's shoulder. The Aussie saunters out of the studio while the German shuts the door and approaches me.

"Where do you want me?" he asks. "I have never taken part in a photo shoot before."

"Don't worry. I'll walk you through it." I wave toward the backdrop I'd set up earlier for Chip. "Stand in front of that and remove your shirt, please."

Benno grins with boyish delight. "Anything you want, I will do."

Oh, jeez, more flirting. If every guy who walks into this studio hits on me, it's going to be a long week. Well, at least I know Dominic won't do that.

I take shot after shot while Benno flexes his muscles, gives me sly smiles, and strikes poses he seems to think are irresistible. He looks kind of silly sometimes, and I suggest different ways he can show off his physique. Benno is more of a handful than Chip had been, and by the time our session ends, I need a break. Luckily, I don't have any other sessions until tomorrow.

On his way out, Benno pauses to clasp my hand and kiss it. "Have dinner with me, Chelsea."

"Um, sorry. I don't date clients." Maybe that's a rule I invented five seconds ago, but I'm desperately trying to let him down easy.

"Anything you desire, I will give you."

"I appreciate the offer, but I have to say no."

Benno sighs, releasing my hand. "If you change your mind…"

"Uh-huh. Goodbye, Benno."

He sighs again, with more melodrama this time, then walks out the door.

The men I photographed today clearly love the spotlight, unlike Dominic. Convincing him to go along with the half-naked calendar idea might prove to be my toughest task.

I'm wiped out, which means it's time to quit for the day.

Avery and Hugh set me up with a swanky flat for the duration of the charity project, so at least I'm going home to comfy conditions. They also offered to provide an on-call limo to ferry me wherever I need or want to go, but I declined. Taxis are good enough for me. I'd feel weird riding around in a big limousine by myself, anyway.

The building where my flat resides features an elevator that I swear has gold leaf on the walls. Not sure I'll fit in here. I'm not a gazillionaire, after all, though I've met one. Diana Sangster is a British billionaire and one of the main sponsors of the cancer benefit and the calendar.

I've just flopped onto the sofa and ditched my shoes when my cell phone rings. I say hello without bothering to glance at the caller ID.

"How was your first day of photographing cricketers?"

"Dominic, it's you." My pulse might have sped up a teeny bit when I heard his voice, but I have no idea why that happened. I guess I'm relieved to talk to a man who won't hit on me, after dealing with Chip and Benno today.

"Yes, it's me, Chelsea. Were you waiting for someone else to ring you?"

"No."

"So, how was your day?"

"Fine. I met Chip Martel and Benno Hochberg." I tuck my feet under me and gaze out the picture windows. "Those two are characters, for sure."

"I've never met Chip or Benno, but I've heard they both loved their celebrity status and missed it when they retired."

"Oh, yeah, they love attention. I lost count of how many times they hit on me today."

He goes completely silent for several seconds.

"Are you still there, Dom?"

He clears his throat. "Yes, I'm here. If those blighters harass you again, let me know immediately."

"They aren't blighters. I think they're basically nice guys under that flirtatious exterior. Benno invited me to dinner, but he didn't get annoyed when I said no."

"You are doing a job. Those wankers shouldn't pester you for dates."

Why is Dominic getting bent out of shape about this? It was nothing.

"It's inappropriate." His voice has gotten growly. "You need a chaperon anytime you are going to be alone with strange men."

"What? That's ridiculous. I've been photographing strangers on my own for ten years, and I'm a big girl who can take care of herself."

Now he literally growls, like an irritable dog. "How many times have you photographed naked men with no chaperon?"

"Never. Benno and Chip were shirtless, not naked. And I don't appreciate your tone. What happened to sweet Dom, the man who's been my friend for years?"

He falls silent again, for even longer this time. "I'm sorry, Chelsea. No idea why I got angry. But I honestly do worry about you."

"I know. That's very sweet, but working with retired cricketers isn't any different than going on a blind date. You never got upset when I did that."

"Ah, well... Never mind."

I can't interpret sentence fragments. All I can do is change the subject. "I'm starving, and I haven't had time to shop for groceries. Want to hit a pub with me?"

"Of course. I'll text you the address to my favorite pub and meet you there in an hour."

"Perfect. See you soon."

I take a quick shower and dry my hair, but I don't bother with makeup. Having dinner with a friend means I can stay relaxed and casual. Jeans and a T-shirt will suffice. Dom and I have been friends for too long for either of us to give a hoot about dressing up to have dinner at a pub.

Dominic told me to meet him in an hour, so I get on my computer to take a quick look at the photos I took today. I can definitely find one good shot for each man. Chip and Benno would look great wearing anything, which made my job easier. Once I've finished browsing the photos, I don't think about either of those men again.

No, I'm thinking about Dominic. I like spending time with a friend, that's all. And I haven't seen him in person for at least three months.

As I walk into the pub, I scan the tables and the bar until I spot a familiar figure sitting alone in a booth. Dom notices me and smiles, waving for me to come to him. I smile too and hustle over there, taking a seat opposite him. His gorgeous brown eyes seem to shimmer in the subdued lighting, and the way he swept his dark hair back tonight reminds me of a young Elvis.

"You must be famished," he says, "after wrangling randy cricketers."

"Not upset about that anymore, huh?"

He winces. "I'm sorry about the way I behaved on the phone."

"Let's forget about that and enjoy dinner. What's good here?"

He aims a devilish smile at me. "What do you think? You're in England, in a pub, so…"

"Fish and chips."

"Exactly. You can order something else if you like, but I will have to call a copper to arrest you for committing a food crime."

I can't help smiling as I shake my head. "Well, I guess I'd better obey The Dom. Fish and chips it is."

"You know I don't care to be called The Dom anymore. I'm no longer a cricketer."

"Once a cricketer, always a cricketer. That's what you used to say."

He sinks back against the booth and groans. "Can we just eat and not discuss that ruddy game?"

"Sure."

Dominic gets a waitress's attention and orders for both of us. "We'll have fish and chips, and a pint for each of us."

I don't usually like it when a man orders for me, but I've always loved it when he does that. Somehow, Dominic manages to sound considerate and sweet when he takes control of my meal and beverage choices.

The waitress brings our beers right away, and we enjoy a friendly conversation while we wait for our food. We do not discuss *that* project. I've decided to give Dominic a reprieve on talking shop, but only until after we've eaten. We sip our pints and laugh a lot, the way good friends should, and he tells me a funny story about his cousin Poppy Goodburn and her bookshop. Once our food arrives, we talk less because we're busy chowing down.

We've just started our second round of beers when I decide it's time to broach the forbidden subject and risk making Dominic growl again. Actually, I kind of liked hearing him growl. That's weird, and I refuse to think about it anymore.

"Put down the chip, Dom," I say. "We need to talk about the calendar. You can eat the rest of your fried potatoes after."

Chapter Three

Dominic

I drop my chip so fast that it bounces off the edge of my plate and falls onto my lap. I use retrieving it as an excuse to avoid responding to what Chelsea said. She wants to talk about the bloody calendar. *Bugger me.* I'd rather discuss the contents of an autopsy report.

"Don't look at me that way, Dom."

"What way?"

"Like I suggested you should try mud wrestling with an alligator."

I shift uncomfortably on my seat, and I'm probably wincing. "That almost sounds more appealing than what you did suggest."

"Why? Going shirtless isn't pornography."

"Maybe not. But posing for, ah, 'beefcake' pictures makes me rather uneasy. I'm not a model."

Chelsea studies me for a moment with an expression I've seen many times before. It means she's figuring out how to sweet-talk me into doing what she wants. "You are a gorgeous man, Dominic. In the whole nine years I've known you, I have never seen you shy away from anything."

"No one has asked me to become a preening male model before."

"You don't need to preen." She picks up a chip and taps it on her lips, then points it at me. "You're overthinking this. Just relax, be yourself, and have fun with it."

Maybe I am overthinking her proposition. I can't help that the idea of being photographed for a calendar isn't something I ever imagined I'd do. The word 'beefcake' unsettles me, though I can't explain why. It's only a word. Women won't be devouring me.

Chelsea has never asked me to do a favor for her. Never. I owe her more than I could ever explain, since she talked me into accepting a job at a girls' school after my cricket career was killed by a knee injury. If Chelsea hadn't encouraged me, I might have turned down the coaching position. Letting her photograph me is the least I can do to repay her.

But I'm still unsettled by the prospect.

"Remember that time you tried to climb up the Tower Bridge while it was being raised?" Chelsea asks. "You only got ten feet up it before you slid back down. Then a cop showed up and gave you a stern talking-to."

"I did that strictly because you told me that only a few people have done that. Then you dared me to try it."

"Dared you? All I said was that John Wayne had been the first actor ever to climb up the Tower Bridge while it was being raised. Hardly anyone has done it since." She points her chip at me. "You decided to show off."

"What does a stupid stunt have to do with your calendar?"

"Because that stunt proves you are not shy. There must be another reason why you're uncomfortable with the beefcake thing."

She might have a point. But I can't do what she wants. Why can't I? No bloody idea.

Chelsea slides that chip halfway into her mouth, then seals her lips around it. She glides it in and out, in and out.

For some bizarre reason, my groin tightens. I shift about in my seat, though that does nothing to alleviate my discomfort. When she bites off a chunk of her chip and chews it slowly, almost sensually, my cock jerks. *Fuck.* What is wrong with me? I've known Chelsea for ages, and I've never reacted to her this way.

Well, maybe once or twice. In my dreams at night. But wet dreams don't count.

It might've happened more than once or twice.

She finishes devouring a fish finger and leans forward. Her voice takes on a huskier tone. "I realize you're a virgin, in terms of posing for professional photos. But I'll walk you through the experience and make sure you feel completely at ease."

Now my breaths have grown shallower and quicker. I feel myself getting hard too. This is insane. Chelsea and I are mates, nothing more. All right, maybe we kissed once. That was ages ago, and we both realized immediately that we're meant to be friends, not lovers.

Chelsea picks up a piece of fish and breaks off a small bite. She chews it the same way she had consumed her chip, turning it into a strangely sensual action.

I knock back the rest of my beer in one mouthful. Then I catch the waitress as she walks by our booth and ask for another pint. I glance at Chelsea, noticing her glass is almost empty. "Would you like another?"

"Sure."

Once the waitress trots off to get our pints, we both occupy ourselves with eating. That only distracts me for a moment since I had two chips left on my plate. Chelsea keeps her gaze aimed at her plate while she gnaws on a piece of fish and shoves chips into her mouth.

The waitress brings our pints.

I down mine in three large gulps.

Chelsea drinks half of hers. Then she fans her face. "Whew, I'm feeling the buzz already."

"That was your second pint. Sorry, I shouldn't have ordered you another."

"Why? It's really good beer."

"But you're tipsy. I swear I wasn't trying to get you drunk." No, I meant to get myself drunk.

Chelsea lifts her glass, puckers her lips, and sets the pint down again. "Maybe you're right. I've had enough."

"Let's grab a taxi, so I can take you home and get you in bed."

She stops blinking, her gaze pinned to mine.

"Oh, bollocks," I say. "I swear I didn't mean that to sound like a come-on."

But the thought of Chelsea lying nude on a bed flashes through my mind. All right, it was more of a lingering visual than a flash. I blame the beer.

I pay our tab and grasp Chelsea's arm, urging her to get up. She doesn't wobble as we leave the pub, but I know she's at least a bit tipsy. She drank two pints while I had three, but the alcohol would affect her more since she's smaller than I am. While I hail a taxi, I need to employ more willpower than seems rational to stop myself from looking down her blouse. Is it my fault she's shorter than I am and that means I have the perfect angle at which to view her cleavage?

Once we've climbed into the taxi, I ask, "Where are you staying while you're here in London?"

"Avery and Hugh rented a flat for me." She rattles off the address.

As the vehicle pulls out onto the street, I instinctively drape an arm across the seat behind her. She rests her head on my shoulder. Maybe it's the beer, but I experience a warm sensation in my chest, and without thinking about it, I curl my fingers over her upper arm. This does feel nice. With the top of her head tucked under my chin, I can smell the faint, almost sweet scent of her hair. Must be the shampoo she uses or…something.

I bend my head just enough that I can inhale that aroma more deeply. Chelsea lifts her head at the same instant.

And our lips brush against each other.

For a moment, we stay frozen with our mouths a hair's breadth apart, our lips parted as if in anticipation of a kiss. I do want to kiss her. It's insane, and I shouldn't want to do that, but my body has other ideas. I feel blood evacuating my brain to flood south, and soon I will develop an erection. Chelsea's eyes have darkened, thanks to the dilation of her pupils, and her lips have turned a richer shade of dusky rose.

Chelsea swipes her tongue across her lips, her gaze locked on my mouth.

It's the beer. It has to be. We haven't suddenly become attracted to each other after nine years as mates. But my breathing has become shallower, and a sizzling current of anticipation races over my skin. I need to taste her, in every way imaginable.

"Here you are," the driver announces. "You lovebirds can get cozy in your flat now."

Lovebirds? No, that's not us.

Chelsea pulls away and opens the door, jumping out of the taxi like she thinks it might swallow her whole.

I lean forward to speak to the driver. "I'm walking my friend up to her flat, then I'll need you to take me home."

He winks. "Whatever you say, mate. Looks to me like you'll be staying here."

"No, I won't."

While I slide across the seat to get out of the taxi, I studiously ignore the smirking driver. Let him think what he likes. I am not shagging Chelsea. We go into the building and take the lift to the second floor and the flat Hugh and Avery provided for Chelsea. At the door, she turns around and leans against the jamb.

"Dinner was nice," she says. "I wish we could see each other more often."

"So do I. Phone calls and video chats aren't enough."

Chelsea settles a hand on my chest. "I agree."

"You could move to this side of the pond. A photographer can work anywhere, right?"

"Mm-hm." She walks her fingers up to the unhooked top button on my shirt. "I'm feeling very…warm and tingly."

Her finger grazes my skin. And my cock jerks. That's my only excuse for what I do next.

I pin her to the doorjamb, then seal my mouth over hers. A thrill rushes through me, as if I've done something wicked, something I should never, never do. But I can't stop myself. I rest my arm on the wall and grasp her hip, tugging her lower body into me, and I slip my tongue between her lips. They feel soft and supple, and her mouth tastes like nothing else on earth. I can't describe the flavor, but it drives me mad, to the point where I know I won't stop until I've consumed her.

She throws her arms around my neck and moans. But when she hooks one leg around my hip, I know I'm about to blow past a line I should not cross, because if I do, I might ruin our friendship. In a minute, I'll stop. I swear I will.

But I seem incapable of doing that. Instead, I slide my hand up to her breast, groaning at the feel of that lush mound cradled in my palm. Chelsea rubs herself against my cock, which threatens to harden into an erection any second.

I tear my mouth away from hers and stumble backward a single step. "Sorry. I, ah, shouldn't have done that."

She seems dazed.

Bloody hell. What have I done? If this destroys our friendship, I'll never forgive myself. So I finally do the right thing.

"Go inside, Chelsea. Sleep off the beer."

Rather than doing what I said, she reaches for me. Her smile is sensual and a touch off kilter.

"Where's your key, Chelsea?"

"Key?"

"The thing you use to open the door to your flat."

"Oh, that." She tries to open her purse but winds up dropping it on the floor. "Whoops."

I grab the little bag and yank the zipper open, then root about until I find the key. While she still leans against the jamb, I open the door. Since it seems unlikely she'll move on her own, I pick her up and carry her into the flat. The door to the bedroom is open, so I take her in there and drop her onto the bed.

For several seconds, I stare at her. She's still fully clothed. I decide I should at least remove her shoes, and after that, I find a small blanket to lay over her.

Then I rush out of the building.

During the ride to my home, I try not to think about what happened and what the ramifications might be. I manage that feat only by studying the view out the window of the taxi. But once I've crawled into bed, the memory resurfaces.

Chelsea's lips. Her body. The way she moaned. The taste and smell of her. No matter how hard I try, I know one fact is inescapable.

I will never forget that kiss.

Chapter Four

My tongue has mutated into cotton, but I can still taste Dominic even fourteen hours after he left me at my flat. I don't remember crawling into bed. Since I'm still wearing my clothes from last night, and there's a fleece throw draped over me, I assume I didn't get myself home. Dominic must have carried me in here.

I vaguely remember the taxi ride.

A shower rinses out the icky feeling of sleeping in my clothes, but coffee resurrects me from the land of the dead. Unfortunately, it also clarifies my thoughts enough that I suddenly recall what happened in the hallway last night.

Dom kissed me.

And I kissed him back.

Holy shit. We're friends, which means we don't grope each other and thrust our tongues into each other's mouths. But damn, that kiss had been so deliciously good, like the most decadent dessert and the best booze in the universe. Dominic intoxicated me, for sure. But he's one of my closest friends, and I never want to lose that.

What if I tanked our friendship?

Maybe Dominic won't remember what happened. Sure, he probably developed total amnesia about last night. I can't worry

about that right now because today I have another session with
a former cricketer. Breakfast revives me even more, especially
since I go to a café that's just down the street and order enough
food to feed an entire cricket team. Well, okay, not quite that
much. But I do pig out on waffles, crepes, and bangers and
mash.

I really shouldn't have thought the word bangers. Not that
Dominic and I did any banging last night. But I wish we had, and
that fact no longer bothers me as much as it should.

Seconds after I jump into a taxi and rattle off the address
of my temporary studio, my phone warbles. It's Dominic. My
pulse revs up, and I suddenly feel a touch woozy. This is ridiculous. We're both adults, and we can deal with our one semi-
drunken mistake.

"Hello, Dom."

"Good morning, Chelsea. How are you feeling?"

"Not hung over, if that's what you're worried about."

He clears his throat. "I wasn't concerned about that. I meant
what sort of happened in the hallway."

"Oh, that." Why am I acting like I had no idea what he
meant? It's nerves, I guess. "Forget about it. That was…one of
those things."

"Shouldn't we talk about it?"

"No need. We're adults who haven't done anything wrong, but
that thing we did last night will never happen again."

"If that's what you want."

Does he want something else? I should ask, but I can't make the
words come out of my mouth. They're lodged somewhere between
my brain and my throat.

"Are we forgetting about it, then?" Dom asks.

"I think that's the best option. Don't you?"

"Sure, I suppose it is." He hesitates, then sighs. "Do you still
want me to pose for that calendar?"

"Yes. You are one of the best-known cricketers in the UK, possibly the world."

He chuckles. "I think you overestimate my fame."

"Are you sure you want to do this?"

"I am. When do you want me?"

Why did he have to phrase his question that way? When do I want him? Right now, naked and on top of me. *No, no, no, he's just a friend, remember?* Yes, absolutely, that's all he is.

The taxi has just pulled up to my destination. As I pay the driver, I tell Dominic, "I've got a session this morning. Why don't you come this afternoon? Say, two o'clock?"

"I have a job, remember? Not just a cricket coach, but a maths teacher too."

"Right. Sorry, I forgot. How about four o'clock?"

"Perfect. I'll see you then."

"Bring your cricket gear."

I spend the morning working with another cricketer who isn't as enthusiastic as Benno or Chip, but Hugo Carter is much more cooperative than Dominic. I get really good shots of Hugo, and I know everyone will be happy with how the calendar turns out, even though I've only photographed three men so far.

While I take shot after shot, I keep thinking about Dominic. About last night. That kiss. His lips on mine, and how good that felt. Despite being a little tipsy, I got turned on so fast and so powerfully from that one lip-lock. Neither Hugo, Benno, or Chip can hold a candle to Dom. He has the perfect physique.

Stop thinking about his body, moron.

I don't understand why one kiss has knocked me for a loop. But I don't have time to worry about that. I go out for a quick lunch, then return to my studio to go through the images I've captured so far and decide which ones I'll use for each man. After that, I take a walk to explore this part of the city, though a solo walk isn't as nice as taking a stroll with a friend.

I know Dominic prefers the country, anyway. He hadn't felt that way before his injury, but after taking a job at a rural private school, Plitherington Girls' Academy, he came to love the quiet and relaxation of the country villages. I'd love to live in a quaint little town too someday.

Now it's time for my session with Dominic.

For reasons I can't explain, I go into the bathroom to check my hair, like it matters whether my hair is messy. I didn't bother with makeup. This is work, not a date.

Someone knocks on the door.

My heart beats faster, and I fluff my hair unconsciously. Then I rush to open the door.

Dom stands there in well-worn jeans and a gray T-shirt, looking hot and casual at the same time. He holds a plastic bag in one hand, which I assume contains his cricket outfit. Dominic gives me an almost shy smile. "I'm as ready as I'll ever be."

"Gee, don't get too excited." I wave for him to come inside. "Stand in front of the screen."

"What screen?"

"Go over there and you'll see."

Dominic shuffles across the floor to the area where I've got everything set up for the photo shoots. But he moves behind the camera, peering through the lens.

I push him away. "That's my spot. You belong in front of the camera."

He winces. "Still not sold on that idea, but I'll give it a go for you."

"Thank you, Dom. I'm glad you're participating, even if it's not entirely of your own volition."

"I would do anything for you."

While I try to figure out if he meant that literally, Dominic moves in front of the camera and turns his back to the screen positioned in front of the wall. Saying he would do anything for me must have been hyperbole and just one of those things people say. Nobody actually means that they'll do *anything* for someone else.

"Should I wear my cricket kit?" Dominic asks.

"Not yet. I want shots of you in regular clothes first."

He twists his mouth into an uncomfortable expression. "Am I meant to take my shirt off now?"

"Yes."

He takes hold of his shirt's hem and lifts it so gradually that I start to wonder if time has actually slowed down. But finally, he pulls the shirt off over his head. Dominic grips the garment in one hand while glancing around. "What should I do with this?"

"Your shirt? Just toss it wherever."

Dominic hurls his shirt. It lands on the floor behind me. "Now what?"

"Try to relax and not look like you've got a metal pole up your ass."

He shifts his weight from one foot to the other several times while wincing again.

Oh, boy. I've got quite a task ahead of me to convince him to loosen up for the camera. "Take a deep breath and exhale it slowly. Look at me, not the camera. That's right. In, out, in, out. You're doing great, Dom."

"I feel like a ruddy fool."

"Come on. You have a great body and a gorgeous face. The camera will love you." Maybe I need to try a different tactic. While I adjust the camera settings, I ask him, "How are your parents doing? I haven't seen them in quite a while."

"They're happy and healthy."

"I'd love to see them while I'm here in England."

"Mum and Dad adore you. I know they'd love to see you too."

He has already loosened up considerably just from our brief, innocuous conversation. My distraction technique is working. So, I keep going with it. "Do you remember the day we met?"

"Of course. My cricket team went to America to play a match for charity against the US team. I'd never been to America before." He cocks one hip, clearly without realizing it, and I click the shutter to catch that pose. "We met in a coffee shop, when you were shocked to see anyone ordering tea."

I wag a finger at him. "No, I wasn't shocked. I'd never met an actual British person before, that's all. It was so cute the way you asked for a 'cuppa,' like Americans have a clue what that means."

"After nine years, I think I've finally trained you in the proper way to order and drink tea."

"Yes, I obey The Dom."

He gives me a sly smile. "I don't mind obeying your commands."

I click the shutter to capture the look on his face. "Wanna see what I've got so far?"

"What you've got? We haven't done anything yet."

"Already took several shots of you."

His brows hike up. "But I didn't hear any noises coming from your camera."

"It's digital, and I turned off the fake shutter sound. Thought you might be more relaxed if you didn't know I was photographing you."

"You sneaky little chit." He smiles again, but this time the slyness has a distinctly sensual undertone. "I had no idea you could be so underhanded, but I like it."

"I've been a photographer for ten years. You are hardly the most difficult subject I've ever had." But he's definitely the sexiest man on the team, hands down. "Come over here, and I'll show you what I've got."

He saunters over to me and slants in to view the images as I flip through them on the camera's little screen. "Can't tell for sure if I should be embarrassed. The piccies are too small."

I can't squelch my snorting laugh. "You Brits have the weirdest way of talking. Hearing a big, brawny man talk about 'piccies' is adorable."

"Just show me the pictures, please. On a larger screen." He pronounced the word pictures with exaggerated care. "I want to know if I should destroy your memory card.'

"You will like the shots, I promise."

I remove the camera's card and lead him over to the desk, where I have a laptop connected to a large monitor. Dominic sidles up to me while I bring up the images. He scrunches up one side of his mouth when the first picture is displayed. But as I flip through them, that expression melts away.

He scratches the back of his neck. "Well, I guess these aren't awful."

"They're good, admit it."

"*You* are good, Chelsea."

"Thanks. But even a hack photographer could get fantastic shots of you." I glance at him sideways. "Ready to see the last shot? It's the best one by far."

"Show me."

I bring up the last image, the one that shows him smiling in that sly, sexy way. He has his hip cocked and his head tipped down just enough to make him seem even hotter.

Dominic tips his head side to side. He has a neutral expression at first, but that gradually transforms into a look of pleasant surprise. "You are a genius. No one else could have made me look this good."

"Bullshit. Why won't you accept that you're smokin' hot?"

He straightens and points at the screen. "Do you have all the shots you need?"

"I'd like to get more, if you're okay with that."

"All right."

Standing this close to a shirtless Dominic, I'm beginning to feel warm all over, and my nipples have tightened. Last night, my body awakened to the possibilities of getting it on with him. And now I'm dreaming up some very naughty ideas.

"What are you thinking?" he asks.

"I have some radical ideas, but only if you're game."

"Tell me."

Chapter Five

Dominic

Chelsea has a radical idea? It must involve our photographic session, but I can't imagine how that could become extreme. I've already taken my shirt off. Maybe she wants me to wear my cricket kit now, but that doesn't strike me as radical.

"Get in front of the screen again," she says. "Then I'll explain my idea."

I do what she asked. "Now what?"

Chelsea bites her upper lip while roving her gaze over me from head to toe and back again. "I know you haven't been fully committed to the calendar idea. But I want to spice it up a little. Here with you. Strictly as an experiment. If the result isn't what you're comfortable with, I won't use those shots."

"You still haven't explained what you want me to do."

"The calendar needs to inspire people to buy it, and the money from those sales will help support cancer research."

"I know that already."

She skims her gaze over me. "Let's make sure the calendar sells like hotcakes—by making it genuinely, mouthwateringly irresistible."

"That's still too vague. What *precisely* are you asking me to do?"

"Let's start slow, so you can get used to the idea." When I open my mouth to speak, she raises her hand to silence me. "I think you'll respond to my radical idea better if you let me guide you through the phases."

Not sure "phases" and "radical" are the sorts of words I want to hear right now. But I trust Chelsea, and I know she won't do anything to humiliate me. "All right. Let's try phase one."

She rakes her gaze over me yet again. Her focus on my body is making me randy, which is not how I want to feel right now. Sure, we kissed last night. I wanted to shag her right then, but I managed to snuff out that impulse. It's wrong. We're mates, not lovers. But if she keeps biting her lip and devouring me with her eyes, I might forget all the reasons why I shouldn't fuck her on that desk behind her.

Chelsea digs about in her purse, then brings out a small bottle. "This is phase one."

I narrow my gaze on her. "What are you planning to do with that?"

"Rub it all over your chest and arms."

"Why?" The idea is arousing me even more as we speak, but I need more information.

She approaches me, halting inches away, and licks her lips while staring at my chest. "This is coconut body oil. I keep some in my purse in case my skin gets dry. You know how itchy I feel when that happens."

"But you want to put that rubbish on me, not yourself."

"That's right. The oil will give your skin a nice sheen that will highlight your muscles and drive women wild."

"What if I don't want them to go wild?"

"Afraid that's inevitable." She taps the little bottle on my chest. "You said you'd try my radical idea. It's for a good cause."

How can I say no? "Fine, give me the bottle."

"I should do it. You aren't a photographer, after all. I know exactly how to slick you up for the camera."

"Just do it already. Make it quick."

"Can't rush. You need to have a uniform sheen."

Never in my life would I have guessed I'd wind up in a photographic studio with a woman telling me that I need to have a "uniform sheen." Never imagined I'd pose for a calendar either. No one else could have convinced me to do this, only Chelsea.

She unscrews the bottle and pours a small amount of oil onto her palm. Then she rubs her hands together. As she lays her palms on my upper chest, her tongue darts out to moisten her lips. I stand perfectly still, because I somehow think that might prevent me from getting an erection. How did last night change everything? One kiss shouldn't have turned me into a ravening beast, but I'm fighting the urge to pull her close and thrust my tongue into her mouth.

With both hands, she spreads the oil over my skin, making a slow, circular motion across my chest. She pours more oil onto her hands, then covers my biceps with the shimmering liquid. It feels warm, probably from the body heat of her hands. Once she's coated my arms from shoulder to wrist, she gets more oil and rubs it over my entire belly.

She takes half a step back. "Turn around. I need to do your backside too."

Her voice has become huskier.

My cock has woken up, but I do as she commanded and desperately try to ignore the signals my own body sends me. Those would be the "shag her now" signals. Might as well be a bloody flashing sign over my head declaring, "Dominic must tear Chelsea's clothes off immediately."

She repeats the process on my backside, massaging that silky, warm oil all over my skin. "Turn around again, please."

Oh, yes, her voice has become even sultrier.

I clear my throat, as if that will help. "What should I do now?"

She scuffles backward, tipping her head side to side as she studies me. "This looks good. Let me get a few shots in before we move on to phase two."

"How many phases are there?"

"Depends on how far you're willing to go for a good cause."

The hairs at my nape stiffen. Am I excited or terrified by her statement? Can't say for sure. The coconut scent of the body oil arouses me more than I expected, and I'm having trouble thinking clearly. As I watch Chelsea walk behind the camera, I seem incapable of wrenching my focus away from her swaying hips and that sexy arse.

Maybe I had noticed her body before. But I'd always dismissed that interest as nothing of consequence. Despite last night, and what's happening right now, I know we will always remain just mates.

I grasp the back of my neck, tipping my head back a touch, and shut my eyes. Yes, we are mates only.

"Perfect," she says. "Try cocking your hip too."

"What are you talking about? I haven't done anything."

"Sure you have. Now, tip your head back a little more, and this time, open your eyes a little."

I freeze. Chelsea took a picture of me just now? I thought she'd give me a warning first. But I do what she told me. I can barely see her through my slitted eyelids.

"Oh, Dom, that was fantastic." She's bending over—to check her shot, I assume—and she peeks at me over the top of her camera. "Why don't you unhook the button on your jeans?"

"Excuse me?"

"Unhook that button. Please."

How can I resist her request when her voice has turned even more smoky and seductive? She can't be trying to seduce me. Chelsea wants a good shot, that's all. And for reasons I cannot explain, I unhook that button.

She rubs her lips together, her gaze nailed to my waistband. "Drag that zipper down a teeny bit. Please."

The tingle I'd experienced at my nape a moment ago suddenly spreads through my entire body.

"Go on," she purrs. "Tug it down."

I draw the zipper down one inch. When she nibbles on her bottom lip, I drag the zipper further down, exposing the top of my shorts.

"Hold that pose, Dominic."

"But I'm still grasping the zipper pull."

"Exactly." She focuses on the little screen on the back of her camera while she presumably takes more pictures of me. After a moment, she lifts her gaze to mine. "I've got an even hotter idea."

"What is it?"

"Take everything off." She holds up a hand. "Hear me out. You undress, but then hold your cricket shirt over your groin to hide your privates."

"Why?"

"Follow my orders, Mr. Rigby, and strip."

"I don't know…"

She tips her head to the side. "Do you trust me, Dom?"

"Yes. But you're asking me to pose in the nude. Some of my mates might have enjoyed dabbling in the naturist lifestyle when they visited America, but I've never done that."

"Not asking you to become a nudist. I'm suggesting you show off that mouthwatering body in a way that will be sure to convince every woman on earth to buy a copy of this calendar. Your manly parts will be covered."

Manly parts? No one has ever referred to my cock that way. As much as the idea of posing virtually nude makes me antsy, I can't deny that it's also turning me on. Because of Chelsea. The look on her face. I'd wager all the money I have that she's as randy as I am.

She walks up to me, tipping her head back so our gazes intersect. The pink tip of her tongue darts out to wet her lips again. "Just think about how much money we could raise for cancer research. Your body can do that."

I wish Chelsea weren't speaking in that sultry tone again. It makes me flash back to last night.

She lays a hand lightly on my chest. "What do you say? Will The Dom show those other cricketers how it's done?"

Will those blokes be upset when they find out my pictures are different from theirs? Well, maybe they'll be jealous that Chelsea asked me to strip, not them. "I'll do it."

Her lips kink up into a wicked little smile. "You won't regret this."

Chelsea returns to her camera but faces away from me.

And I strip. Then I grab my cricket shirt, holding it in front of my groin. "All right, I'm ready."

She turns around, and I swear her tits are rising and falling more heavily. "Need more oil."

"That's not a good idea."

"Oh, it absolutely is."

I wait while she grabs the bottle and slathers coconut-scented oil over my lower body, though she avoids my groin. The shirt covers it. The sensation of her hands rubbing me down threatens to drive me insane, because I'm experiencing an overpowering urge to do things I swore I'd never do.

Chelsea rises slowly, her attention riveted to my body. "Time for some test shots." She hurries back to her camera, keeping her head down. After apparently taking some pictures, she peeks up at me through her lashes. "Throw the shirt over your shoulder and shield your manly parts with your cap."

I wish Chelsea would stop saying "manly parts." Not because it annoys me. Because she keeps talking in that sultry, hungry tone. But I do what she asked. While Chelsea shuts her eyes, I sling the jersey over my shoulder and retrieve my cap to hold it over my cock. The hat essentially covers my growing erection, but it might not for much longer.

"I'm ready, Chelsea."

She opens her eyes—and they go wide. "Wow, Dominic, you look so damn hot. We'll sell a million copies of the calendar, at least."

"Aren't you forgetting something?"

Her lids flutter, as if she's coming out of a trance. "What?"

"You're meant to be taking pictures of me."

"Oh. Right." A nervous laugh bubbles out of her. "Almost forgot I had a job to do."

She focuses on her camera again. Though the camera makes no sound, I can tell every time she clicks the shutter button because her eyes narrow for a second.

"Get on your knees," she commands, without looking away from her camera.

I fall to my knees.

She snaps more pictures. "Now, get rid of the cap and hold the shirt down there instead."

Once I've done that, she takes more images. But after a minute or two, she looks at me—well, at my groin. Why? Because I now have a raging erection.

"Chelsea, you need to stop staring at my cock."

"Looks like there's a cobra under that sweater and it's rising. Can't see your dick."

"Are you disappointed?"

She gazes straight into my eyes. "Yes, I am."

I drop the shirt.

Chapter Six

Chelsea

I am staring at Dominic Rigby's dick. My mouth has actually begun to water, and I feel tingly from head to toe. He dropped the sweater. Maybe I sort of complained that I couldn't see all of him, but I never expected him to show me his dick. I hadn't been thinking clearly then, and I still can't manage to do that. My body wants me to mount him. Or for Dom to mount me. Either one will work.

He cups his erection. "Don't stare at this unless you want me to go over there and take you on the desk."

Do I want that? Hell yes. But it's a horrible idea. Well, okay, it's the best idea I've ever heard and I want it so badly that I can't catch my breath. Dominic is my friend, and I shouldn't risk our friendship for one incredible fuck. What if it's not incredible? Bad sex would wreck our relationship for sure.

Dominic saunters up to me and shuts off the camera. "I think we're both experiencing the same thing. Aren't we?"

Oh, yeah, we are. Sizzling, molten, pure unadulterated lust. But I can't speak, so I simply nod once.

"I don't want to destroy our friendship," he says. "But I can't deny that I'll go mad if I don't shag you right now."

"Yeah, I feel that way too."

"How should we handle this dilemma?"

I shrug and shake my head.

Dominic rubs his jaw. Then he smirks, and his eyes sparkle. "I have a brilliant idea."

"About what?"

"How to deal with our problem. I've been celibate for far too long, and that's probably why I want to shag you. I think you've been celibate too, haven't you?"

"Yes. For way too long."

"We both work hard and don't have time for dating."

"I know. What's your brilliant idea?"

He moves closer, bending his head until it hovers inches away. "Let's do each other a favor, now and then."

"Huh?" Lust makes it hard to concentrate on his words, but the closeness of his oil-slicked body makes it impossible.

"I said let's do each other a favor. Every time we feel the urge, we'll get together and satisfy each other's needs." He rubs his thumb across my bottom lip. "No strings. Just sex."

"How would that work? I mean, where would we do it?" Why am I asking? It's crazy. I can't have casual sex with Dom. Can I?

"We should have a few rules, to keep it casual. No kissing, no holding hands, no beds, no hotels." He inches closer, and I feel his dick brushing against my belly. "Whenever we need a pick-me-up, we arrange to meet somewhere that's not my house or your flat. The more inappropriate the location, the better."

"I don't understand. Why is an inappropriate place better?"

"Because it will be hotter. We'll have cracking shags every time when we're being naughty."

Getting naughty with Dominic sounds way too good. I can't do this. But I want to do it. God, do I want to. A long, long dry spell has turned me into a crazy person, for sure, and I don't care. "Yes, let's do each other a favor. As needed."

Yeah, it's kind of like a prescription. One hit of Dom as needed to scratch that itch. Am I mixing metaphors now? Oh, who cares. I need an orgasm so badly. Dominic Rigby has the body and the sensuality to make that dream come true.

"Did you say yes?" he asks. "Not sure if I imagined that."

"You didn't hallucinate. Let's do it, Dom."

"Right now?" The heat in his voice could melt steel. "On this desk?"

"Please, yes, now."

"Do you want to undress, or just pull your trousers down?"

"Whatever's fastest."

He unzips my jeans, shoves his fingers inside the waistband of my pants and undies, then yanks it all down to my ankles. The clothes gets caught on my shoes, essentially binding my feet. Dominic hoists me up to set me down on the desk. "Last chance to back out."

"Not backing out. I want this. I want you."

Dominic pushes his body between my thighs only far enough that the crown of his cock grazes my cleft. "I can already smell the scent of your cream, and I'd love to feast on you. But I think that would violate the terms of our agreement."

"Yeah, it probably would." I suck in a breath when he rubs his crown over my clit. "I don't have a condom. Please tell me you do."

He freezes, and his expression goes blank. Then he scrunches up his face and hisses, "Bollocks."

"I'm on the pill, but we should still use a condom. Shouldn't we?" Part of me hopes he says we should screw that. Okay, maybe most of me wants to say that. I'm so drunk on lust that I can't think straight.

Suddenly, his disappointment vanishes—and a naughty smile curves his lips. "Oh, I have another brilliant idea."

"I loved your first brilliant idea, so whatever it is, go for it."

He tugs me closer until the very edge of my bottom rests on the desk and his firm dick lies nestled between my folds. The crown nudges my opening. I think I know what he plans to do, and the thought alone makes my clit pulse.

"This will be hard and fast," he says. "Celibacy hasn't improved my willpower."

"Quit talking and fuck me already."

He rubs his length up and down my cleft, taking it slow at first, but quickly escalating the pace until his dick is scraping up and down, inflaming my need so much that my slick flesh becomes even more swollen and sensitized, triggering a hot tingling everywhere that his cock touches me. I grip his biceps and squeeze my eyes shut, so overwhelmed by the sensations that my breaths become sharp gasps.

Dominic shoves his hands under my ass. The movement pushes his erection even more firmly into my cleft, and I can feel his crown pushing into my opening just enough that it drives me out of my mind. I wrap my legs around his hips, throw my arms around his neck, and let him take full control of my orgasm. My pulse has gone into overdrive, and I feel a little lightheaded, but I don't care.

He pauses only long enough to reposition his dick so the crown is nudging my clit.

I need more of him, all of him, and I can't stop myself. I thrust my hips wildly.

"Bloody hell," he growls. Then he tips forward until my back meets the desk, with his body still plastered to mine. "Can't last much longer. Need to make us both come right now."

"Yes, yes, please."

He squeezes one hand between our bodies and begins to massage my nub. I go off so fast and so hard that my entire body goes rigid, and I can't produce any noises, not a scream, not even a whimper. White-hot pleasure scorches through me as I squeeze my eyes shut once again and let the climax rush down every nerve, across every inch of my skin, like a wildfire incinerating the landscape.

Dominic lets out a strangled shout and freezes.

Then it's over.

I lie here dazed and stunned, struggling to comprehend what we've done. Nope, I'm not there yet. A massive dose of hormones has turned my brain to mush.

"Bollocks," Dom hisses. "I've made a mess of you."

"Huh?" I peel my lids apart and blink several times before the world around me comes back into focus. "What did you say?"

"I've made a mess of you, that's what I said." He nods toward my lower abdomen. "Do you have a change of clothes?"

"Uh, no." I push up on my elbows to gaze down at my belly. Some kind of wet, milky substance has stained my shirt. And I abruptly realize what he meant. "You came all over my shirt."

"Yes." He grimaces. "Sorry."

"Don't apologize. That was fantastic." Now that my brain has resumed mostly normal behavior, I hold out my hands to him. "Help a girl up, hey?"

"Yes, of course." He grasps my hands and helps me into a sitting position. "I swear I can do better than this. It's been so bloody long since I had sex that I've lost my finesse."

I can't help laughing. "You've got plenty of finesse. And the next time one of us needs a favor, we'll both do a lot better."

"You want to continue with my plan?"

"Sure."

The actual, completely honest answer sounds more like "whoa, mama, holy shit, hell yeah, yes, yes, yes." I haven't had sex in a long time either, and I feel like fist-pumping and whooping. But I restrain myself.

Dominic bows his head, screwing up his mouth. Then he peeks up at me through those thick, dark lashes. "This wasn't how I expected my first photo session to go."

"I don't normally screw my subjects."

"We didn't actually shag. It was more like mutual masturbation."

"Did the trick, though, didn't it? We had orgasms."

He shuffles over to where he'd dumped his clothes on the floor and pulls them on again. Rather than sitting down to put his shoes and socks on, he hops around on one foot, then the other, to get the task done.

A poorly squelched laugh snorts out of me. "Are you practicing for your debut as a drunk ballet dancer?"

He straightens and rests his hands on his hips. "Are you going to harass me after every time we do each other a favor?"

"Maybe. If I didn't harass you, then you'd know we strayed over that invisible line."

"Fair point." He glances at the backdrop screen. "I think the session is over for today. Will you want me again?"

"Yes. I might want your body in front of the camera again, if that's what you meant."

"It is. But if you need my body for other reasons, let me know right away."

"You can't drop everything to have sex with me. All day long, you're working—at a girls' school."

That naughty smile returns, even wickeder than before. "I said we should shag in any inappropriate place we like. The school has a janitorial closet, among other things. Be spontaneous, Chelsea, and creative too."

"I like the way you think, but I've never been adventurous with sex."

"Time to break the rules." He stretches and groans as if he's extremely satisfied. "I'm starving. Let's find a pub."

"Good idea. I'm ravenous too, but I need more than fish and chips after what we just did. I'd love some steak followed by an extremely fattening dessert."

"I know a place." His attentions drops to my chest, and he grimaces again. "You can't go out looking like that."

"Mind if I wear your sweater?"

He grins. "That's perfect. But only if you call it a shirt. You are in England, after all."

Dominic turns away as I start to lift my shirt's hem. That's an oddly respectful thing to do, considering we kinda sorta had sex a few minutes ago. I strip off my dirty shirt—yeah, that statement now has a double meaning—and shrug into the shirt. It's sized for Dom, which means it's baggy on me. I swear I can smell him on the fabric. That's dumb, though. He must have washed this thing since the last time he wore it. But I haven't seen him in his shirt since the last time he participated in a professional cricket match.

That was eight years ago.

While we make our way down to the street, I can't resist asking him a question. "Have you worn your cricket shirt since you quit the pro circuit?"

"No. Why would I?"

"Because it's yours."

"I have no sentimental attachment to my shirt. It's nothing but a piece of clothing."

We climb into a taxi, and Dominic tells the driver to take us to a different pub this time, one he tells me offers hearty steak dinners twice a week. Luckily, this is one of those days. During the ride to the pub, I keep thinking about what happened in my studio and what we agreed to do on a regular basis. We didn't have intercourse, but we did share a sexual experience. It was beyond incredible.

But can we really keep it casual?

Chapter Seven

Dominic

Once we reach the pub, I try to forget about that "favor" we did for each other in Chelsea's studio and force myself to focus on eating. The food is excellent. I wolf down an entire ribeye steak and a large mound of mashed potatoes, not to mention a pile of mixed veggies. I always have a strong appetite, but I rarely consume a meal so quickly.

In the wake of our "photo session," my appetite now involves more than food. Much more. As I hack off another bite of steak with my knife, I can't stop my mind from treating me to a replay of what we did on Chelsea's desk.

Stop thinking about it or you'll get hard again.

To stave off an embarrassing situation, I watch Chelsea eating. She normally makes use of every utensil and chews with delicacy. Not tonight. She's eating like she just finished competing in a triathlon, shoving large chunks of steak into her mouth and gnawing it to bits with no regard for decorum.

Oddly, watching her makes me randy.

She must have a culinary black hole in her mouth because I see no other way Chelsea could have any room in her stomach for dessert. But she devours her meal, then wolfs down a large slice of apple pie too—with ice cream. All of that was accompanied by a pint of bitter.

When she reaches for her mug, about to raise it and ask the waitress for another drink, I yank it away from her. "You'll make yourself sick."

She puckers her lips, gazing hungrily at the mug. Then she sighs. "Yeah, you're probably right. One pint of beer is enough."

"Glad to hear it."

"You ate as much as I did, but you're a large, brawny man. I have no excuse."

What does the fact I'm a "large, brawny man" have to do with anything? Chelsea must still be reeling from our sort-of shag.

I finished eating before she did, so I witnessed it every time she shoveled pie and ice cream into her mouth. As I recall seeing that, my lips twitch in a slight smirk. "You weren't exaggerating when you said you're ravenous."

"Nope. I always tell the truth."

"I know. You are the most honest person I've ever met." I lean back, folding my arms over my chest. "If you're going to react this way every time we shag, I'll need to hire a personal chef to keep you fed."

"Just hand me a tub of ice cream. That's all I need." She pushes her empty plate away. "Well, that and condoms. We absolutely must go all the way next time."

"I agree. And I guarantee that next time I will have a large supply of condoms."

Talking to Chelsea about sex and protection feels a bit strange but also exciting. I might need a favor from her every day. I definitely need to see her naked, completely naked, because our pseudo-shag set off a chain reaction that led to incredible pleasure, and the reaction hasn't dissipated. It simmers away inside me, ready to erupt at any moment we want. Maybe I should sprint to the nearest pharmacy and buy condoms, strictly so I can be sure I'll have them when they're needed. I don't want to forget.

And I need to be inside her next time.

That doesn't mean anything. It's lust, pure and simple.

I insist on escorting Chelsea to the door of her flat, and without thinking about it, I kiss her cheek when we say goodbye. I don't think I've ever done that before. She seems a bit confused. Well, I'm feeling confused too. What is wrong with me? I was being polite, that's all. I shouldn't try to ascribe any special meaning to a brief peck on the cheek. One amazing sexual experience together hasn't changed my feelings or hers.

Once I get home, I go straight to bed and sleep so well that I wake up in the morning refreshed and ready for another day of teaching young girls how to play cricket as well as how to do maths. Though I honestly do love my job, coaching is not for the faint of heart. Those girls give me as much of a workout as they get.

While I shower and get dressed, for reasons I can't understand I start thinking about Chelsea and all those other blokes she'll be photographing. At least two of them flirted with her. What about her session today? Will that wanker hit on her? She might like it this time. Maybe she'll accept a date with him.

Oh, bugger me. Now I'm obsessed with which imaginary cricketer will ask Chelsea out on an imaginary date. Then they might develop an imaginary relationship and eventually have imaginary children.

I've lost my mind. Maybe work will help me find it again.

Just as I climb into my car and shut the door, my mobile rings. The screen tells me who it is, and I rush to answer, nearly dropping my mobile. "Good morning, Chelsea."

"Are you okay?"

"Yes. Why wouldn't I be?"

"Well, we did, um, do that thing yesterday. Thought I should check on you. Make sure you aren't feeling weird about it."

"I feel fine. Are you all right?"

"Sure, yeah."

Her tone seems a bit too breezy, which makes me wonder if she's the one feeling weird about our halfway shag last evening. "I'm about to leave for work. I'm in the car, actually. If you want to talk about that thing, we could meet for lunch."

"No more pubs. Beer impairs my judgment more than I realized."

She can't mean that beer made her do something she normally wouldn't. We were both dead sober, as far as I knew. We didn't have a pint until after our halfway shag.

"No pubs," I say. "We can dine in no-star luxury at my usual haunt."

"What does that mean?"

"The school cafeteria."

After a lengthy pause, Chelsea says, "Okay. I'll meet you in the cafeteria at noon."

"It would be better if we met in the car park. You've never been here before, and the halls are sort of like a maze."

"Really? That sounds intriguing."

"No, it actually isn't. But I'll explain when you get here."

"I'll see you at noon."

We say goodbye, and I get on the road. I don't live in London since Plitherington Girls' Acadmey is in a rural area twenty minutes from the city. Working in the country never used to appeal to me, but since I retired from pro cricketing, I've realized I love the quiet and solitude.

But that solitude only lasts until I arrive to work.

The start of a new school year means a new crop of girls. I'll have two groups of cricketers to deal with—eleven to thirteen, and fourteen to sixteen. Those are the only ages who attend Plitherington. I do not look forward to the first day with a new group of cricketers. It's usually chaos. At least the older group have already mastered the rules and most of the techniques.

After checking in at my office, and responding to all my emails, I head out to the cricket field. I always arrive well in advance of when the girls will show up, to make sure the equipment is there and in good condition. Last year, a teenage boy had sneaked onto the campus to meet his girlfriend and impress her with his cricketing skills. The daft teenager managed to break a bat. Nothing like that will happen ever again. The school installed cameras throughout the grounds.

The equipment is all accounted for and in working order.

Our cricket ground is nothing more than a large, well-mown grassy field with a long bare strip in the center, flanked by the wickets. We don't have a stadium or even a proper playing area. Maybe I do occasionally miss the pro circuit, when I competed in full-size stadiums with sold-out capacity. Hearing the cheers when I swung my bat and the ball went flying… Yes, I do miss that sometimes. As for the deafening roar whenever I knocked the ball so high and far that everyone had to run to catch it, but they missed and my team won… Yeah, I sometimes miss that too. A lot. There's no greater high than winning.

No, that's not entirely true. Watching Chelsea come was the best high I've ever experienced. I need to shag her all the way next time.

A horde of girls, all aged between eleven and thirteen, pour out of the building and rush onto the field. Each of them wears their cricket kit. I'm standing on the pitch waiting for them, and I raise a hand to halt the girls.

"Stop there," I announce. "You don't get to step onto the pitch until I say so. First, you need to learn the rules and get used to the equipment."

The girls express their disappointment in varied ways, everything from slumping their shoulders to pouting. Then they finally take a good look at me, and their expressions brighten. Can't imagine why. Maybe they're excited to learn the game. The girls begin whispering and exchanging secretive smiles, some of which are aimed at me. I've seen this reaction before, but it always baffles me.

One girl thrusts her arm up and waves her hand while grinning. "Mr. Rigby! Mr. Rigby!"

"What is it?"

"Can I be your assistant? I could pick up the bats and balls after every practice session."

Assistant? I've never had one of those, and I don't care to have a schoolgirl scurrying after me. "What is your name, pet?"

"Hillary Markham."

"Well, Hillary, I appreciate the offer. But you're meant to learn the game, not play rubbish collector."

She bows her head and pouts.

Another girl squeezes past the others to get in front. "My sister Cynthia will be playing on the fourteen to sixteen team this year. She had you last year too, and Cynthia swears you're the hottest coach ever and she wishes you'd take your shirt off."

I stare at the girl. Her sister said what? Why is this child telling me that? I did not need to know that Cynthia thinks I'm hot. But that's one of the sticky issues that come up occasionally when a bloke works with young girls. I've gotten used to it—mostly.

"Why would Mr. Rigby take his shirt off?" another girl asks. "That's not regulation kit."

"Cynthia says—"

"Enough," I shout, only loud enough to get their attention. "Girls, you need to focus on learning the game. Forget about whatever Cynthia might've said. Listen to me and do everything I say. Understood?"

A chorus of "yes, Mr. Rigby" ripples through the group, and they finally settle down to await my instructions.

I spread an arm to indicate the area directly behind me. "This entire area is the cricket field, and the area directly behind me that has no grass is the pitch. How many of you have played cricket before?"

None of them raise a hand.

"Have you watched a cricket match?"

Several girls raise their hands.

"Do you know the fielding positions and the rules? Or at least which area is the infield and which is the outfield?"

Every hand falls back down. I suppose it was too much to hope that one or two might have a modicum of experience. Watching cricket isn't the same as playing the game.

"All right, we'll start from the beginning," I say. "Once you've mastered the basics, you'll have the chance to play a practice match. Eventually, you'll take turns with the various fielding positions."

A girl opens her mouth, undoubtedly to ask how long it will be until she can do what I suggested.

I raise my hand. "Be quiet and listen."

She closes her mouth.

Children are obeying me. That doesn't happen as often as I'd thought it might when I first took this job. I've learned a lot about how to tame excitable children, and apparently, that experience has paid off at last.

I pick up one of the balls I'd left on the ground with the other equipment. "Your first task is to master the use of this ball. How many of you know what a wicket is?"

All but six of them raise their hands.

I rest my free hand on my hip as I roll the ball in my palm. "Not all of you will make it onto the team. This initial phase will help me identify the best players. Some of you might serve as substitutes, meaning you will only participate in a match if a teammate is injured or unwell. The rest of you will be cut from the team."

And now the real work begins.

Chapter Eight

Chelsea

This morning, I'm doing absolutely nothing. Another former cricketer was supposed to pose for me today, but he needed to reschedule for personal reasons. That leaves me with a big blank spot in my work schedule. What should I do? I'll meet Dominic for lunch at his school at noon, but it's only nine o'clock now. Driving to Plitherington will only take twenty-seven minutes, according to the map thingy on my phone. Will Dominic mind if I show up early?

I try to call him, but I get his voice mail. He must be busy teaching math or coaching budding cricketers.

Though I'm used to living alone, being in another country by myself is disconcerting. I need to do something. Sightseeing? That's not much fun alone. Museums? Also more fun with a friend. I call Avery but she's working with one of her image consulting clients today. I've met a lot of Dominic's buddies over the years, but I don't know them or their wives very well. The only real friend I have in this country is Dominic.

Maybe I could surprise him at work. Say I need another favor? Since we did that last night, I can't decide if today is too soon for another round of hot casual sex.

After pacing in the living room of my flat for twelve minutes, according to my phone, I give up. I'm bored, and nothing will perk me up as quickly or as spectacularly as a quickie with The Dom. But I can't call in a "favor" fourteen hours after we got down and dirty in my studio. I should wait a respectable length of time first. What's respectable when it comes to sexual favors?

Oh, who cares. I'm going to Plitherington right now.

I rush downstairs and hail a taxi, but the driver informs me that nobody would agree to drive me that far outside the city unless I want to pay "a ruddy fortune." Twenty-seven minutes doesn't seem like that far to me. My morning commute back home takes at least twice as long as that.

The cabbie agrees to drop me off at the nearest "car hire" agency, so I quickly rent a compact model and order the map thingy on my phone to lead me to Dom's school. The trip only takes eighteen minutes. *Huh.* Did I drive a little faster than I should have? Maybe. Not sure why I did that. I can't be *that* excited about screwing Dominic again.

I blame the dry spell I'd experienced before yesterday. Yeah, that's the reason.

As I pull into a parking spot in front of Plitherington's main entrance, I suddenly remember I'd promised to call Dominic when I got here. I climb out of the car and lean against it while I dial his number.

He answers on the sixth ring. "Chelsea? Do you need to cancel our lunch date—I mean our lunch appointment?"

Nice backpedaling, Dom. But I don't say that out loud. "Not canceling. I'm here."

"Where?"

"In the parking lot. I know I'm way early, but my only photo session for today got canceled. Is it okay that I'm ahead of schedule?"

"Of course it is." He pauses. "I'm happy you're here. But I have a bit more coaching to do with these girls this morning."

I really should have called before I took off on my little road trip. Dominic has a job, and his work hasn't gotten canceled for the day.

"Are you still there?" he asks.

"Yes, I'm here."

"Why don't you come out to the cricket field? You can observe my coaching skills, such as they are."

I glance around. "Not sure where the field is."

"As you're facing the building, you'll need to go around the left side. Once you round the corner, you'll see a large grassy area with a clay pitch in the center and wickets too."

"Those are the upright thingies at either end of the pitch, right?"

"Yes. How can you not know the cricket jargon after all these years of being friends with me? You attended matches too."

"Yeah, but all those terms are weird and confusing. Some players are called 'silly,' which makes no sense."

He sighs heavily. "Not sure if we can still be mates when you refuse to learn the secret language of cricket."

Dominic spoke those words in a deeper tone, and my body thinks I need to get turned on right now. That's the last thing I need.

I weave through the cars in the parking lot and trot around the building until I see the carefully mowed cricket field. I swear I can smell that fresh-cut grass. Maybe I'm not hallucinating. They might have mowed the grass yesterday in preparation for the start of the new school year.

That fresh green scent sticks with me as I cross the field, halting far enough away from the pitch that I shouldn't be in danger of getting whacked in the head with a ball. These kids must be newbies, when it comes to cricket, so I doubt they can throw as far as Dom could. I've seen him in action, back when he was still on the pro circuit. Hearing the crack of the bat when he struck the ball and watching it soar through the air had been so damn sexy.

Dominic glances my way and smiles. "You can come closer, Chelsea. We're about to learn the overarm throw."

I jog up to the gaggle of girls who loiter alongside the pitch.

Dom strides over to grasp my hand, dragging me in front of the gaggle. "Girls, this is my good mate, Chelsea Vance. She's here strictly to observe, so let's all be on our best behavior."

A blonde girl sighs and slumps her shoulders. "You have a girlfriend?"

"Chelsea is my mate, not my girlfriend. But that's none of your concern." He turns to me. "Stand wherever you like, but I recommend keeping a reasonable distance from the pitch. We're using soft balls, but they're still, ah, not something you want to take a hit to the face from."

"I'll back away."

While I do that, the girls keep casting me a wide array of disappointed looks. I had no idea there were so many ways to express that kind of sentiment. These kids are talented in that respect, but can they throw a cricket ball?

Dominic picks up the ball and tosses it back and forth between his hands. "Listen up, girls. You've already done your warm-up exercises. Now it's time to get acquainted with the ball. This one is soft, so you can get used to it without knocking each other's teeth out."

A brunette thrusts her arm straight up and flaps her hand.

Dom gives her a patient smile. "What is it, Carina?"

"Do we need to take notes?"

"No, pet, you don't. After this introductory session, I will provide you with reading materials so you can practice on your own."

Carina lowers her arm, but she and the other girls keep gazing at Dominic adoringly while he explains the two types of throws—overarm and underarm. I can't blame those girls. He is gorgeous. Dom has an incredible body and a sexy voice, not to mention a beautiful face. I remember with vivid detail what he looks like naked and how good it felt to have his cock between my thighs.

I need to go all the way with him so badly.

Ugh. I shouldn't be thinking about that.

Dom tells the girls that he will demonstrate both types of throws but only after he explains about wickets and bails. Despite the fact I've heard that speech before, when we first met and he told me all about his favorite sport, I still don't get that stuff about wickets and bails. I'd never been interested in sports, but after getting to know Dominic, I came to appreciate cricket. Maybe I just like watching athletic men with good bodies hurl balls and whack them with bats.

After regaling the girls with his wicket speech, Dom begins his lesson on throwing. He stands sideways to the pitch and raises his arm, the one holding the ball, then bends his elbow. He rocks backward right before leaning forward to release the ball. It flies across the pitch and sails over the wicket at the other end.

His speech did not clear up the wickets issue. Is it just me, or do all Americans have a special gene that prevents us from understanding British sports?

I observe while Dominic demonstrates how to bowl, or throw the ball, and how to bat. Each girl gets comfortable with the overarm method pretty quickly. Then Dominic teaches them how to bowl the underarm way. After that, he turns a learning experience into a game, making it fun by letting the girls earn points by mastering each type of throw and how to catch the ball once it's flying through the air. The girls have a great time, and learning to bowl involves plenty of laughter.

"At the end of the month," Dom says, "the player with the most points will earn a prize."

He really knows how to motivate kids. I've seen Dominic in action on the cricket field, during professional games and when he played with friends. But until today, I had never seen him teach. He is amazing. Those girls love him, and not only because of his looks. They clearly appreciate his style of coaching and the nuggets of cricket wisdom he offers, all based on his experience in the world of professional cricketing.

"Quiz time, ladies," Dominic announces. "Who can name all the catching methods and the types of balls?"

A red-haired girl waves her hand with great enthusiasm.

Dominic nods to her. "Share your wisdom, Cecily."

"There are overhead, chest-level, and ground balls. The types of catches are orthodox cup, high catch, and low balls."

"Excellent. After school, go home and practice everything you've learned today, preferably with a mate."

The best part of watching Dominic teach these girls is how much I'm learning about him in the process. He must be an amazing math teacher too. Anyone who can wrangle a bunch of preteen girls and turn them into proper cricketers would definitely rock the classroom too. I wonder if I could sit in on one of his math classes, just to watch him work. Watching him coach makes me unbelievably horny. I want to drag him into the woods and do the naughtiest things to him. So, I probably shouldn't visit his classroom. I might get too lustful for public consumption.

Soon, it's time to end the coaching session. Dominic gives a brief speech, telling the girls how well they all did and how proud he is of the way they took to the game. The smitten students listen to every word. Even when he tells them that next time they'll be learning the rules of the game and will need to practice hard to get good at cricket, they still adore him.

"See you on Wednesday," Dominic says. "Now, head for the cafeteria. It's lunchtime, ladies."

The girls trot off toward the building.

As the last stragglers disappear through the doors, Dominic walks over to me. "How did you like it? Coaching isn't as exciting for spectators as a real game is."

"I disagree. You are an impressive coach, and I loved watching you mold those kids into solid bowlers and catchers."

"We don't call them catchers. Are you here for lunch?"

"That's what we talked about doing."

He moves closer until less than a foot separates us. "But is that what you want right now?"

The huskier tone of his voice ripples a hot shiver through me. I'd been turned on already after watching him work, but now I can see the sweat that's soaked into his shirt and the way that fabric clings to his muscular body.

Dom inches even closer. "How hungry are you, Chelsea?"

"Ravenous."

"Again? Are you hungry for food, or something else? Last time you said you were ravenous, you wanted fish and chips."

What do I want? I suddenly realize I've leaned toward him and tipped my head back to gaze into those beautiful brown eyes. Their color reminds me of rum, and they intoxicate me just as much as any booze might. Maybe that explains what I say next.

"I need a favor, Dom."

Chapter Nine

Dominic

I stare into Chelsea's eyes, unable to move or look away, transfixed by the desire in her eyes and her expression. She traces her tongue over her bottom lip, then nibbles on it, while her attention stays focused exclusively on my eyes. I want to kiss her, but we agreed not to do that. Keep it casual, that had been my idea.

Now she wants a "favor." My cock loves that idea. But there is a problem.

"This is a school," I say. "We can't shag on the cricket pitch."

"Are you saying two intelligent people can't figure out a way to screw each other on school property without any of the kids seeing us?" She hooks a finger inside my waistband and tugs. "Besides, you suggested getting it on in the most inappropriate places."

Of course I did. Somehow, I forgot about that when I saw the lust in her eyes right now. But I don't care to be arrested for exposing myself in front of schoolgirls.

Suddenly, the solution hits me.

I sling an arm around Chelsea's waist and crush her body to mine. "I left my car at the far end of the car park, under a large tree that offers plenty of shade. That means shadows."

"Are you suggesting sex in your car?"

"Yes. I have condoms in the glove compartment."

She grins. "Let's do it."

I claim her hand, leading her away from the field. Our swift walk becomes a sprint. We've both been celibate for too bloody long, so naturally, we get a bit excited by the prospect of a quick, hot shag. What we did last night was fantastic, but I need to sink my cock inside her this time.

Everyone is in the cafeteria right now, so we don't see any other people. But the idea that someone might catch us fucking in my car makes me even more excited. I think it's affecting Chelsea the same way, since her cheeks are pink and she keeps grinning at me.

At the car, I stop to consider the options. "Backseat or front?"

"You got a new car. A smaller one."

"Is that a problem?"

"Not sure we can both fit in there. We might kick out the windows without meaning to."

"Oh ye of little faith." I yank the front passenger door open, then lean in to pull the lever that makes the seat tip backward. I push it all the way back. "See? Plenty of room."

"Uh, you're way bigger than I am."

I pat her arse. "You can be on top."

Her lips curl into a sly smile. "You are naughtier than I ever realized. I like it."

"This will be my first experience with automotive sex." I retrieve a condom from the glove compartment and climb in, lying back on the reclined seat. It's more comfortable than I would've thought. "Get on top of me, Chelsea."

She clambers onto my body, straddling my hips, and pulls the door shut. I follow her movements as she undoes the tie on my boxer shorts and loosens the waistband. Then she tugs the shorts down past my hips and groin.

My cock jumps up, like it can't wait to fuck her either.

Chelsea gazes down at my erection, licking her lips. "Mm, can't wait to have you inside me."

"Unbutton your shirt, love. I need to at least see your tits."

She frees the buttons on her shirt one by one, taking her time, teasing me with the promise of what I'll see at any moment. I know what her lower body looks like, but I desperately want to get a look at those breasts. I'd love to hold them in my palms and taste their tips too.

Her shirt falls open, but her bra still impedes my view.

Then I notice something. "Is that a front-close bra?"

She nods.

"Allow me, then." I release the first of the tiny clasps that hold the bra together. "Can't believe how excited I am to see your tits."

"I'm aching for you to see them. Touch them. Fondle them."

My hands tremble while I release another clasp, then another. Only two more to go. How can I be this desperate just to see another part of her body? It's barmy, but I don't care. As I free the last clasp, and her breasts tumble out of the constraint, I swear my mouth actually waters. *Blimey.* She has the most beautiful tits I've ever seen. I can't resist cupping them in my hands. Her skin feels like silk, and those rigid peaks beg for me to touch them.

I massage her breasts until she bites her lip, then flick my thumbs over the nipples.

Chelsea gasps.

One touch is not enough. I slide my hands around to her back and pull her closer until her tits dangle over my face. I catch one taut peak between my teeth and suckle it.

She gasps again.

I push a hand under skirt. Blue knickers cover the part of her I need to touch so badly, though I need to sink my length into her silky heat even more. I try to rip her knickers off. It doesn't work. I've never tried to tear a woman's underwear off, but in the movies it's always easy to do. Reality is disappointing.

"Bloody hell," I growl. "Can't get your knickers off."

She tries to remove them herself, but the close quarters complicate the task. She nearly kicks me in the face while trying to wriggle out of her underwear.

"Glove compartment," I say. "Should be a pocket knife in there."

Chelsea twists around to yank the glove compartment open and dig around until she finds what we need. She hands me the pocket knife. I flip it open, hook the small blade inside her waistband, and slice her kickers in half. She tears them off and tosses them onto the driver's seat. Then she smiles. The expression is filled with so much lust and excitement that I can barely breathe.

I reach for the condom she holds in one hand.

But she closes her fingers around it. "Uh-uh-uh. I'm going to do this."

"That's not a good—" I groan as she rips the condom packet open and begins to roll it onto my cock. "Not a good idea."

"Why not?" She keeps rolling the condom down my length, little by little, as if she means to torture me this way. "You seem to like it. Your pinched expression proves that."

"Maybe it is the best sort of torture, but I might come before you even get me covered."

"Oh, I think you've got iron willpower. Any man who can teach preteen girls how to play cricket without yelling at them or resigning from his job can handle what I'm doing."

"Just hurry, would you?"

Chelsea finally finishes her task. Then she rises to her knees, positions my cock, and slides down onto it.

Another, deeper grown vibrates in my chest.

She rocks gently. "Oh God, this feels so incredible."

"Yes, it does. But please move faster. My iron willpower is melting."

I grasp her hips while she rocks faster and plants her hands on my chest. With her eyes half-closed, she moans and increases the pace even more, until she's bouncing on my cock while panting and scraping her nails on my shirt. I can't stop myself from lunging my hips up into her movements. The way our bodies collide creates a wet sucking sound, and the aroma of her lust infiltrates me with every breath I take, making me even more turned on. Her tits flap. My growling mutates into grunting. The car begins to shake.

Fuck, I'll come any second. I know it. So I rub her clit furiously while she pummels my cock, gasping and whimpering. Her body freezes. She seems to have stopped breathing too.

This is the moment. She's about to come.

Her inner muscles clamp down on me while I keep rubbing her clit mercilessly, pushing her toward an even bigger climax. I don't know how I do that, but she does come even harder. Staccato breaths burst out of her.

"Yes, Dom, yes! Keep fucking me, never stop, keep fucking me."

I clutch her hips to stop her from rising up and punch into her so hard that the car creaks and thumps. A hoarse shout explodes out of me.

Neither of us moves. My ears are ringing, and all I can do is gawp at her like a moron. My chest heaves. Hers does too. Chelsea's mouth has fallen wide open, giving me a clear view of her tongue. Her body is still wrapped around my cock.

"Holy shit, Dom." After a few seconds, she squints at me and smacks my chest. "I told you never to stop."

"Well, I couldn't reasonably do that, could I? As much as I would've loved to fuck you until the end of the universe." I can pull off only a half smirk. "Even I'm not that good."

She collapses on top of me, her head tucked under my chin. "I thought last night was amazing. But this time was even more unbelievably mind-blowing."

"But we didn't even fog up the windows."

"Maybe next time."

I brush my fingers through her hair. "I'm still inside you, pet."

"Mm-hm."

"Shouldn't we disentangle?"

"Mm-mm."

I love the feel of her body nestled on top of me and her silky hair teasing my skin. Her warmth envelops me. And for the longest moment, I can't convince myself to move. But we did agree to quick shags only, so I shouldn't allow us to revel in the intimacy of post-coital cuddling. Still, it takes me longer than it should, so long that I don't know if I can reasonably call this a quick shag anymore. Yes, the actual sex was fast and furious. What we're doing now is…something else.

"Are you hungry?" I ask. "We just had a workout, and I'm famished."

"Yeah, me too."

"We should, ah, fix our clothes and go into the cafeteria."

Chelsea sighs, then pushes up to straddle me again. She pulls away and reaches for my cock as if she means to peel the condom off me.

I grasp her wrist. "Better let me do that."

"Why? You came, so it'll be quite a while before you can get hard again."

"Usually, yes. But after what we just did—" I wipe a hand across my mouth. "Let me clean myself up, all right?"

"Sure." She clambers over the center console and sits on the driver's seat. "Should I look away? Wouldn't want you to get embarrassed."

"Are you being cheeky? Can't imagine you actually think I'd be embarrassed to have you see my dick when your cream is all over it."

"Yeah, but men can be weird that way." She watches as I remove the condom, then find an empty paper sack under my seat and drop it inside. "Are you really okay, Dominic?"

"I'm fine. Why do you keep asking?" I eye her sideways. "Are you uncomfortable with what we did?"

"No. And that makes me uncomfortable."

I sit up and raise the seat back. "I don't understand. How could you be both happy and uneasy?"

She shrugs. "Emotions don't always make sense. But I guess I'm probably feeling a little weird because now we have to go into the cafeteria and act like we didn't screw each other like crazy a minute ago."

"Isn't the risk of getting caught what makes the pleasure so intense?"

"Yes." She leans closer. "Thank you for the favor, Dom."

Chelsea throws the driver's door open and jumps out.

I get out too and perform a visual inspection of my car. Despite the wild nature of our fucking, the vehicle did not bounce halfway across the car park. I might have thought of that possibility right before we came, but it was only a fleeting thought. Another idea, one I can't get rid of, disturbs me more. The intensity of our lust for each other seems like something deeper than two mates enjoying a casual shag.

No, it's only a favor.

Isn't it?

Chapter Ten

Chelsea

When Dominic and I walk into the cafeteria, everyone watches us, but they act interested rather than surprised. Dominic introduces me to his fellow teachers and the administrative staff, all of whom sit at a long table with us. He calls me his "mate," and everyone seems satisfied with that explanation of who I am. We didn't hold hands on our stroll from the parking lot to the cafeteria. Why would we? We're not dating. Favors only, that's our arrangement.

The man sitting beside me turns out to be the music teacher, and we have a wonderful discussion about that topic. I also chat with the headmistress who sits across from me. Maybe I had weird ideas about British private schools, but I assumed the woman in charge would sit at the head of the table.

My thoughts keep returning to the moments in Dominic's car, when we had given each other the most incredible favor. I couldn't help feeling sort of…closer to Dom after what we'd done. I see no evidence that he experienced the same kind of thing. I'm sure it's only the hormones that still course through my veins. Sex can cause a surge in oxytocin, or so I've read, and that can make two people feel more bonded. I'm not in love with Dominic. Maybe I've had trouble looking him in the eye since we did that favor for each other, but I'm sure the unease will pass.

Then we can go back to being friends, with no weirdness between us.

After lunch, Dominic walks me out to my car. He opens the driver's door for me too. When I settle onto the seat, he leans in. "I have two classes to teach. Then I'm preparing for my first coaching session of the newest crop of teenage cricketers, but they already know the rules and tactics. After that, I'd love to have dinner with you tonight."

"Dinner? Should we really do that?"

"Friends can share a meal. We've done that twice this week." He studies me for a moment. "You are feeling odd about our favors, aren't you?"

"No, no, I swear I'm not." Oh yeah, that didn't seem at all like I was covering. "I'm sorry, Dominic. I think I'm too tired to go out tonight, that's all. Maybe tomorrow?"

"Yes, tomorrow." He gives me a tight smile. "Have a good day."

He shuts the door and heads back toward the building.

And I drive back to my flat. During the whole trip, I keep wondering about how Dominic reacted when I told him I was too tired to go to dinner with him. He probably meant we would go to a pub. Still, he seemed more disappointed than I expected, considering that we aren't dating or romantically involved in any way. I wanted to comfort him, but that would have violated our agreement for sure.

I spend the rest of the afternoon combing through the photographs of the cricketers who have posed for me so far. I'd given those pictures a quick skim this morning, but now I pore over them to choose which ones should be included in the calendar. When I work my way up to the images of Dominic, something strange happens to me. I get turned on, yes, but I also feel a tightness in my chest that isn't unpleasant. And it makes me want to drive to his house and apologize for refusing to have dinner with him tonight.

That's crazy. I didn't do anything wrong, and he can't possibly be offended. I've declined his dinner invitations before, and he didn't care. But I need to make sure he's okay about it today. So I call him.

He answers right away. "Hello, Chelsea."

Well, at least he sounds normal now. "Hi, Dominic. Are you mad that I wouldn't have dinner with you tonight?"

"No. Why would I be angry?"

"Maybe that wasn't the right word. You seemed to have hurt feelings when I said I'd rather stay home."

He doesn't speak for several seconds. Then he sighs. "I'm sorry if I led you to believe I was upset. I'm not."

"Are we okay, then?"

"Yes, we're fine."

"Oh, good." My phone chimes, indicating a new text message. I glance at it quickly. "Avery wants to talk to me. She says it's urgent."

"Hmm. I suspect that's urgent meddling of some sort."

"There's nothing to meddle about with me."

Dominic chuckles. "You haven't spent enough time around my British mates and their spouses to understand the depth of their commitment to interfering in other people's lives."

"Why would they bother with me? I live in America."

He laughs louder this time. "Continents don't matter. You and I are mates, which means they will insist on trying to force a romance between us. It worked on all my other unmarried friends. Chance Dixon, Reese Dixon, Dane Dixon, Richard Hunter, Nick Hunter, Alex Thorne, Diana Sangster. Not so much with Ben Montague. He met Samantha all on his own, and the American Wives Club didn't need to interfere."

"The American what club? I thought your friends were all British, anyway."

"Yes, they are. But Alex's true love is Scottish."

Good thing I'm already sitting down, because I'm getting totally confused.

"Let me give you the background," Dom says. "The American Wives Club started in Scotland, when the American wives of the brothers Lachlan, Aidan, and Rory MacTaggart decided to meddle in the lives of other Scots. From there, it spread to England like an unstoppable plague. They've also inducted men into the club as honorary members or as full-fledged members of the British Branch."

I can't speak for a moment. I had no idea his friends had a club for meddling, or that it's so big they needed to create an offshoot. "Are your friends insane? Is this club like an evil organization in a James Bond movie?"

"No, pet, they are not evil or insane. But they are bloody annoying sometimes."

"You think Avery wants to talk to me as an ambassador for this club or something."

"Hard to say. You won't know until you talk to Avery. She's a lovely woman, but don't let her rope you into anything." He lowers his voice to a sarcastic whisper. "Be careful. If they brainwash you, I'll need to hire a team of crack psychologists to abduct you and cleanse your mind."

"Gee, you'd do that for me?"

"Of course. I should buy some camouflage fatigues just in case I need to storm Sommerleigh House."

That's where Hugh and Avery live. Hugh Parrish is the Viscount Sommerleigh, though the etiquette of the aristocracy requires everyone to call him Lord Sommerleigh. Some people call him Lord Steamy, but that's not an official title. I attended Hugh and Avery's wedding as well as the fun events leading up to that day, so I know the Sommerleigh estate is gorgeous.

"I hope a commando raid won't be necessary," I tell Dominic. "But it's nice to know you care enough to deprogram me."

"What else are friends for?"

"I should probably call Avery and find out what she wants."

"Good luck."

We say goodbye, and I dial Avery's number. She answers after one ring. "Chelsea, I'm so glad to hear from you."

"I got your text. Figured you would want me to call. What's up?"

"Hugh and I were wondering how long it will be until you finish photographing the ex-cricketers."

"Um, not sure. I've only worked with three of them so far. That leaves nine more, and I've had trouble scheduling their sessions because of conflicts. They all have jobs."

"Guess they're busy guys." She hums tunelessly, as if she's working things out in her mind. "Let me think on it. I'm sure we can come up with a solution."

"To what? It's only been a few days. Creating a calendar takes a lot of time, and it's too soon to need a solution. There's no problem yet. I can handle it on my own."

"Oh, I wasn't implying you can't do your job. Hugh and I have connections, though, and maybe we can help those guys clear their schedules for you."

I think I'm finally beginning to understand what Dom was talking about earlier. Avery and Hugh must be trying to meddle.

"You should come to Sommerleigh," Avery says. "We had planned all along to have the retired cricketers practice for the big match on the estate grounds. If we invited them to come sooner, like this weekend, you could take some extra shots of the men that might be good for publicity purposes. Sounds perfect, doesn't it?"

"Do you mean instead of shooting the calendar in my studio?"

"No, in addition to that."

My mouth opens, and my jaw just hangs there while I consider what she suggested. "I can't get all these guys to come to my studio this week. Nine more of them? I've had trouble scheduling sessions for three of them."

"Let me handle that. I'm an image consultant, which means I'm an expert on how to manage people. Trust me. By noon tomorrow, I'll have them all booked for you."

That sounds great, but I'm not convinced she can do it. I know Avery is a smart, driven, accomplished woman. But convincing nine cricketers to pose for me this week? That seems like a job for the Impossible Missions Force. Maybe Avery will call in Tom Cruise to help her. "Okay, go ahead and try."

"You will hear from me by noon tomorrow. That's a promise."

After we hang up, I still can't believe she might do what she promised. I've been a professional photographer for too long to believe any job will be a piece of cake.

Oh, great, now I want to eat some cake. I don't have any on hand, though.

The next morning, I do my usual routine—shower, eat, go over my work schedule for the day. But I don't have anything going on unless Avery succeeds in performing a miracle. I won't hold my breath for that. I'm about to leave my flat, headed for my studio because I can't think of anything else to do, when Dom calls me.

Instead of the standard greeting, he says, "Are you aware of what Avery and Hugh have done?"

"I know Avery claimed she could get those nine cricketers to fall in line and pose for me. But I doubt she can really do that by noon."

"No, she did it by before eight o'clock this morning."

"What?" I freeze with my hand on the doorknob. "Was she up all night harassing those guys?"

"She got most of them last evening and the final bloke this morning."

I am literally standing here speechless. My vocal cords have apparently frozen up like an old computer. "That's impossible. I mean, she swore she could do it but—Holy shit, that woman is amazing."

"Yes, she is. There's more, though."

Now my imaginary computer brain is starting to overheat. I think I see wisps of smoke emerging from my ears. "Do I want to know what the American Wives Club is plotting?"

"Probably not. They want—" He mutters what sounds like a curse under his breath, but I can't understand the words. "I'll be late for work if I don't hurry. We'll talk later. Good luck today."

He hangs up.

Yeah, now I have a queasy feeling in my tummy. Dominic said I probably wouldn't want to know what's up, then he said "they want" but never finished the sentence. I rush to my studio in case one or two guys have already shown up there. But when I step out of the elevator onto the floor where I have my studio, I freeze and gape at what I see.

Nine former cricketers. Lined up along the wall. Waiting to get into my studio.

Damn, Avery is my new hero.

Chapter Eleven

Dominic

I should have rung Chelsea again once I got to Plitherington, but I didn't have time. The entire campus is buzzing with the news that I and eleven other former cricketers will not only pose for a calendar but will also play a charity match against eleven of the current best men in the league. Am I ready for that? I haven't participated in a serious match in years. I'm rusty, to say the least. But I promised I would do whatever Hugh and Avery wanted, because it's all to raise money for cancer research.

But now they want the entire team of has-beens to practice at Sommerleigh House. Oh, I have no doubts Avery and Hugh mean to push Chelsea and me together somehow, maybe by locking us in a closet or handcuffing our wrists to a radiator. Chelsea still does not understand the depth of the meddling that the American Wives Club has instigated in the past. They kidnapped Hugh, for pity's sake. All right, he might've deserved that since he'd been acting like a bit of an arse, trying to steal Kate Wagner away from Callum MacTaggart. But abduction seemed like overkill. They could've simply let Magnus MacTaggart, the scariest Scot on earth, wallop Hugh until he gave up.

I'm not afraid of Magnus. I meant that other people see him that way.

All morning, students, teachers, and administrators alike grin at me and whisper to each other whenever they see me. I hear various individuals talking about the calendar because they don't know how to whisper properly. The students are the worst offenders. I swear they're actually batting their eyelashes at me—particularly the teenagers. Today, I'm meant to coach the cricket team for girls age fourteen to sixteen. But I have a bloody awful time keeping them focused. They engage in even more whispering and lashes-batting, but also gaze at me dreamily.

The headmistress informed me that I'm allowed to take whatever time off I need to participate in the charity events. How did she know about that?

Oh, I have an idea how. And I am going to strangle Hugh for this. I would bet my life savings that he notified the school about the charity rubbish. Raising money for a good cause isn't rubbish, but the way Hugh, Avery, and all our mates are meddling is utter, inexcusable rubbish and bollocks and bullshit. I have no proof my other mates are implicated in the plot. But I have good reason, based on previous experience, to believe they intend to interfere in my life and Chelsea's.

By sheer force of will, I convince the girls to pay attention and practice their cricketing skills. All right, I may have growled once or twice. Unfortunately, they seemed to like it. When I threatened to have their cars towed away, the driving-age girls finally started listening to me. The others fell in line after them.

The older girls don't need as much hands-on training with me as the younger ones do. I've only just begun to train those girls, the ones who have never played cricket before, and now I plan on leaving for six weeks. Plitherington has given me permission to do that, but I've never taken so much time off, especially at the beginning of the school year.

I feel guilty. Of course I do. But it's not strictly because I'll be abandoning my students. I want to prove I can still compete against younger blokes on a national stage. Can I do it? Or will I wind up as a large, human-shaped stain on the grass with a cricket ball jammed up my arse? I'll find out in six weeks.

At lunchtime, I walk into the cafeteria—and stop dead just inside the doors. Why? Because a large banner stretches across the room, hanging above the windows.

It says, "Good luck, Mr. Rigby. The Dom rules!"

The entire hall erupts with cheers and clapping.

Bloody hell. Until this moment, I hadn't realized how big the charity match could be. If everyone at Plitherington is this excited, what will happen when the event is publicly announced?

I'm in over my head. But it's too late to back out.

Somehow, I manage to focus on my job and teach my classes in the afternoon. After that, I go home and slump on the sofa, staring at the telly without actually watching what's playing. Maybe I'm taking this charity match too seriously. No one expects me to be the star player. I'm only one of eleven men who will take the field.

Why am I anxious about that? It's ridiculous.

I feel much more relaxed now, so I ring Chelsea to find out how she's handling all those randy ex-cricketers.

"Not as bad as I was afraid it might be," she says. "Though I did I arrive at my studio this morning to find a horde of buff men lined up waiting for me."

"I hope they didn't harass you too much with their flirtations."

"Luckily, six of them are married or have serious girlfriends. So they behaved like normal human beings. The other three hit on me a little bit, but the flirting doesn't bother me."

"Did you photograph all of them today?"

She laughs. "Are you kidding me? I barely got three of them done today. You sat for me, so you should know that I take a lot of shots in various poses to make sure the calendar committee can choose the perfect picture."

"Committee? I thought this was a casual charity event."

She bursts into a fit of raucous laughter. "Where did you get that idea? Hugh and Avery brought in every member of the American Wives Club to engineer this massive, three-part event. Avery told me all about it over lunch today."

"I thought you were too busy to go out to lunch today." Did she simply not want to see me after our car shag?

"Avery can be very persuasive. She took all of us—me and the cricketers—out to lunch at a great pub."

"Oh, I see."

She hesitates, then speaks slowly as she asks, "Do you feel slighted because I had lunch with Avery and the guys instead of with you?"

"Well, no, that would be pathetic." I shift around on the sofa, suddenly unable to get comfortable, and clear my throat. "Are you bothered by what we did yesterday?"

"The car thing? No, I loved that. Are you bothered by it?"

"Not at all."

"Good." Why did I ask her about that again? She already told me she's fine with it.

I shift around some more, and I swear ants have crawled into my trousers. "I know you've had a long day. But would you like to come to my house for dinner?"

"That would be great, but I'm too wiped out to drive."

"What if I came to you? I can bring everything I need to cook you a nice meal."

"Um…" Noises suggest she's moving around, probably the way I'd done a moment ago. "Okay. Come to my flat and feed me."

"I'll be there in an hour."

And I live up to my promise. I knock on the door to Chelsea's flat precisely one hour later. I'd needed time to gather the food items and find a container to carry them in, which turned out to be more difficult than I expected. I'd never brought a load of groceries to anyone's doorstep until tonight.

When I ring the bell, Chelsea flings the door open almost instantly. "Dominic, you're right on time."

"Have I ever cooked for you before? I'm thinking the answer is no."

She shakes her head. "No man has ever cooked for me before."

"Really? You're a man-cooking virgin."

"That might be the dumbest joke you've ever come up with."

"It sounded better in my mind."

She escorts me into the flat and into the kitchen. "I don't have any fancy cooking implements or whatever. I've mostly eaten out since I came here and only had cereal for breakfast."

"Oh, that's no good. You need a hearty meal to sustain you during those long photo sessions." I drop my sack of ingredients on the counter. "Are you sure those wankers aren't sexually harassing you?"

"I'm sure. Mild flirtation only. They're actually nice guys, even Benno."

"Glad to hear it. I was ready to punch all of them, which probably would have resulted in me needing medical attention."

She leans toward me, and her breasts graze my chest. "If that ever happened, I would be the one tending to your wounds. We could play nurse and patient."

"That sounds like a sex game. But you couldn't have meant that."

"Why not? Maybe I need another favor after the hard day I've had."

"My day was exhausting too, for different reasons." To avoid her gaze, I start removing items from my sack of groceries. "The entire school has heard about the charity events, including the calendar."

"I bet those teenage hearts went pitter-patter like crazy when they heard about that."

"There was a bit of eyelash fluttering, that's all." I glance at her sideways. "Did you know our mates have arranged for me to take six weeks off from work? Just so I can practice for the charity match."

"Yeah, I know. Avery told me about that at lunch."

"Am I the only one who thinks this is an insane plan?"

Chelsea rests her elbows on the counter, a position that pushes her arse out behind her. "You're the only cricketer who hasn't embraced the craziness. It's supposed to be fun, Dominic."

"I'm aware of that conspiracy theory."

"Conspiracy? You're being silly."

As I sort through the food items I'd brought, I try very hard not to admire her arse. But the way she's standing there ensures that lovely bottom catches my attention every time I glance at her. I still haven't seen her completely nude. Which does not matter. The occasional favor should be quick and casual, not lengthy enough that we see each other naked.

She knows what I look like without clothing. It doesn't seem fair that I haven't had the same experience.

Casual shag, you ruddy moron. And stop staring at her arse.

"What's really bothering you?" Chelsea asks. "It's got to be more than the calendar or the publicity that might come with taking part in a charity extravaganza."

"Since when did it become an extravaganza?"

She gives me an exasperated look. "What did you think it would be? You agreed to pose for a calendar, attend a gala, and play a cricket match against some of the best players currently in the game."

I've been slicing up a zucchini, but now the knife tumbles from my grasp. "The best players? I thought this was for fun and to raise money. Now it sounds like a death match."

Chelsea sets her hands on her hips. "Okay, enough is enough. Tell me the truth. Why do you get so bent out of shape whenever I talk about the charity match?"

I start to speak, but she jabs a finger at me. "The truth, Dominic."

Sighing, I rub my eyes. "All right. The truth."

"Right now."

"Yes." I grip the counter's edge and stare down at the slices of zucchini. "What if I can't handle competing against younger men who have been practicing religiously? I might embarrass myself and my teammates."

"Are you worried about your legacy?"

"What legacy? I've never been a celebrity. Just an average cricketer."

She sidles up to me. "You honestly believe that, don't you? People still call you The Dom. They wouldn't do that if they thought you were a has-been."

I wince. "The school put up a banner wishing me good luck and declaring that The Dom 'rules.' It's bollocks. I haven't played a professional game in years."

"Once upon a time, you were the most confident man I'd ever met. And you absolutely did dominate the field and earn that nickname." She lays a hand on my arm. "What's changed?"

"Everything. I blew my knee out and had to retire, then took a job coaching girls. My knee healed, mostly, enough that I probably could've played again. But I gave up."

"Why?"

I need to consider the answer to her question for a moment before I know how to respond. "What if I'm not The Dom anymore? What if my knee can't handle the stress and I become permanently disabled? Or worse, what if I'm rubbish at the game now?"

"Oh, Dominic." She wraps her arms around me. Her head rests on my shoulder. "I get why you're worried about your knee, but you did the physical therapy and saw a specialist. They all said your knee is in good condition now. I think you're really worried about humiliating yourself and tarnishing your reputation as The Dom."

"I hate that nickname."

"Because you don't feel worthy of it anymore. Right?" When I grudgingly nod, she hugs me more firmly. "Nobody will think that, and no one will ever take that title away from you. Face it, you'll be The Dom forever, regardless of how the charity match plays out."

"You honestly believe I can do it. Play again after years away from the sport."

"I do. But the only thing that matters is what you believe."

Though I want to scratch my head, I can't do that with Chelsea hugging me and pinning my arms to my sides. "If you believe in me, that's all I need to know."

Chapter Twelve

Chelsea

"Let's collaborate on dinner. You need to relax, Dominic, and cooking will distract your from your worries." I study the food items he has laid out on the counter. "I love zucchini, but I can't figure out what your meal plan is here. You've got canned tomatoes, garlic, pasta, and a few seasonings."

"It's meant to be zucchini pasta with tomatoes."

"What's in that brown paper package?"

"Salmon. I had the other items on hand, but I stopped at the market to get the final ingredient."

I release him and lean forward to peel the paper away from the fish. "I love salmon."

"Yes, I know. That's why I bought some. I thought I'd pan fry the salmon, then crumble it into the pasta."

"Mm, yum."

Cooking with Dominic becomes a fun experience filled with plenty of jokes and laughter. He finally releases all that pent-up anxiety and lets himself enjoy hanging out with me. I love spending time with him, and I wish we could see each other more often. Our lives and careers don't allow that to happen. I've thought about that problem more and more over the past year or so, but I didn't think he ever wondered about that.

Until he proves me wrong.

As we're enjoying our meal on the sofa, at opposite ends, he sets his plate on his lap and looks at me. "We'll see a lot of each other over the next few weeks. But then you'll go home to America."

"What are you trying to say?"

"I'll miss you. I always do when you leave, but lately, I wish we had more time together."

"Me too. But I built a career in America, and your life is here in England."

He bows his head and picks at his remaining food. "You could move here. Once the calendar is released, everyone will know what an incredible photographer you are. It would be harder for me to relocate."

"Why is that?"

"Immigration, visas, figuring out if my teaching credentials would be accepted there."

"Guess it doesn't matter. We're just friends, anyway." I set my empty plate on the sofa between us. "Want to make a quick dessert together? You know, my neighbor across the hall gave me chocolate wafers as a welcome gift, and I bought some whipping cream. Thought I'd put that in my hot cocoa. But this means we have all the ingredients for an icebox cake."

"That does sound good." He winks. "I would love to whip that up with you. Because the recipe involves whipping cream."

"I caught your joke. But it wasn't good enough to earn a chuckle, much less a belly laugh."

"Need to step up my game, eh?"

Dom and I have collaborated on desserts before, so I figured that would be an easy way to give him an out for our conversation. It was clearly making him uncomfortable. I know him well enough to realize he needs to think about important discussions for a while before he can assimilate the information. I can't give him too long, though. He might find ways to wriggle out of finishing our talk.

While we wait for the icebox cake to chill, we watch TV. Dominic wanted to watch a professional cricket match, but I nixed that idea. He needs a break from thinking about all that stuff, so I suggest we watch a documentary about astronomy instead. That's about as far from cricket as we can get.

Sharing a large slice of cake is distracting too. I had wanted to make two pieces, but he insisted on only one. Then I find out why.

He sinks his fork into the cake to peel off a mouthful and hold the loaded tines to my lips. "Ladies first."

"That's a very sexist thing to say. Shame on you." I'm smiling, so he knows I'm kidding.

"Open your mouth, or I'll smash the cake onto your face."

"You're a secret dictator, huh? That's even worse than being sexist." I lunge forward to take the fork into my mouth and moan as he pulls the tines away. My eyes are shut, though I didn't do that on purpose. "This is a truly orgasmic food experience."

I open my eyes and realize Dominic is staring at me, wide-eyed and frozen. *Oops.* I probably shouldn't have used the word orgasmic. He probably thinks I want another favor, and the idea clearly doesn't appeal to him. Or maybe he's just shocked that I would want that again. I'm too tired for sex, though.

"Didn't mean that the way it sounded," I say. "The cake is incredibly delicious, that's all I meant."

"Yes, I could tell you enjoyed it." He takes a bite and makes a sarcastic show of moaning in ecstasy. He even rolls his eyes up as far as he can. "You were right. This is orgasmic."

I snatch the plate away from him. "Guess I better eat the rest. You might have a heart attack."

"Oh, no. You cannot steal the cake I made."

"We made it together."

"I did most of the work." He holds up his hands, palms down. "See how arthritic my poor hands are? It's because of whipping all that cream."

"Now you're just being ridiculous." I break off a bit of cake with my fingers and smoosh it into his lips. "There's your share."

He licks the chocolaty goodness off his lips. Then he grabs a handful of cake and smooshes it into my lips.

I lick it off while his gaze tracks every movement of my tongue. Once I've cleaned off my lips, I grasp his hand so I can wipe the cake and cream off his palm with my tongue.

Dominic is staring at me again with his eyes wide.

Oh, shit. Why did I lick his hand? Maybe I subconsciously want to get him worked up because I love having sex with him. Our "shags" have been amazing. So yeah, it's nothing but horniness.

Dom lunges forward, aiming for my mouth.

I throw a hand up between our mouths before he can claim my lips. "What are you doing? No kissing, remember?"

"Oh, right." He slumps into his corner of the sofa. "I forgot for a moment. Sorry. It was a barmy impulse."

"Yeah, I figured. Don't worry about it."

"Let's watch another astronomy program."

We're both uncomfortable now. Maybe watching a documentary will ease the tension between us. Five minutes into the show, Dominic gingerly slides closer to me. Ten minutes in, he cautiously rests his arm across the sofa's back. Sometime after the twenty-minute mark, I fall asleep. Before I know what's happened, I'm waking up with the morning sun shining through the windows in my bedroom. I lie under the covers, wearing my clothes but no shoes.

I sit up, yawn, and stretch. Then I notice the folded note taped to the lamp on the nightstand. I snatch up the note, which has my name scrawled on it in Dom's handwriting. *Sorry to leave without saying goodnight,* he wrote, *but I didn't want to disturb you. Check the refrigerator when you get up. Yours, Dominic.*

My heart skipped a beat when I read that word—"yours"—I swear it did. But I don't have time to think about why. It's a standard sign-off, right? Lots of people would end a note that way. Right now, I'm more interested in why he told me to check the fridge. If he's pulling a prank, and I get a face full of whipped cream when I open the fridge...

No, he wouldn't do that.

After a quick shower and a change of clothes, I head into the kitchen to find out what Dominic meant with that last comment in his note. The fact that he left me a note is so sweet. He must have carried me into the bedroom too, and that's even sweeter. I've known since the day we met that he's a nice guy, but only this morning have I discovered exactly how thoughtful he is.

I pull the fridge door open. "Dom, you sneaky sweetheart."

He made me a full icebox cake, using a pan I hadn't known I owned. Well, I don't really own it. I'm leasing this flat, and it came fully furnished—with all the necessary cooking utensils. Dominic also left me another note, this one taped to a plate that's covered with plastic wrap. He has created an entire morning meal for me—a full English breakfast. That means bacon, sausage, eggs, grilled tomatoes, mushrooms, fried onions, baked beans, and marmalade with toast. When I read the second note, I learn he left tea warming in a kettle on the stove as well as a pot of coffee on the counter.

I didn't have all that food in my fridge. How did he find time to go shopping and make me breakfast? Glancing at the clock on the microwave, I finally understand. I've slept in until nine o'clock.

"Oh, no," I moan. "No, no, no, no. I'll be late for my first photo session."

Talking to myself doesn't help me claw back the two hours I need to be on time for work. But as I remove the plate of food from the fridge, the note slips out of my hand—and I see more words written on the backside. *I rescheduled your morning appointments,* Dom says, *because you needed more rest.*

I'm annoyed that he commandeered my schedule, but mostly, I want to drive to Plitherington just so I can plant a big wet kiss on him. He took care of me, last night and this morning. How can I be mad at him for that? I eat all the food he cooked for me and text him a message letting him know I loved it. Since I have no appointments this morning, thanks to Dominic's machinations, I take a stroll through the city—the parts within walking distance of my flat—and let myself do nothing except appreciate the scenery.

Dominic didn't provide me with a lunch meal, so I stop in at a café. Now it's time to get back to work.

I photograph three more former cricketers, all of whom had shown up yesterday, so I know who they are. All but one dive into the process with gusto. The outlier shares Dominic's discomfort with the camera, but unlike my friend, he asks for my help in learning how to give me what I need for the calendar. I've coached my fair share of camera-shy people. Coaxing a sexy pose out of one guy is no problem.

Well, as long as the man is not Dominic Rigby. He fought the process longer than any of the other guys, though he eventually gave in. He stripped naked when I asked him to do it. That sweater hadn't hidden everything.

"Are you all right, Chelsea?"

My head pops up, and I stare at the man who spoke. "Yes, I'm fine. Sorry I zoned out for a minute."

Colton Ward smirks. "I'm not electrifying enough to keep your attention?"

"It's not you, I promise."

"Sounds like I need to revamp my efforts." He whisks his pants off, now standing there in only a tight pair of briefs. "Does this do it for you?"

Might as well take a few shots. This is supposed to be a sexy beefcake calendar. But even while I photograph Colton, who has a great physique, I can't muster any real interest in his body. He seems like a nice guy, but I don't have any desire to go out with him either. Colton poses like a pro and gives me plenty of great shots. But when he offers to show me "the full monty," I politely decline.

"That's not necessary," I say. "This isn't a nude calendar. You gave me plenty of material, and I'll have no trouble picking out one perfect image for you."

"Brilliant. Glad I could help out with the fundraising."

Colton might be the only cricketer I've photographed who hasn't hit on me. He made a silly joke about whether seeing him in his briefs "did it" for me. But he hasn't actually flirted. And I just realized he isn't the only cricketer who has never made a pass at me. Dominic didn't do that either. But he did suggest we should do each other a favor whenever we want it.

After two more days of photo sessions, I need to call in that favor.

Chapter Thirteen

Dominic

After my last coaching session of the week—my last for a while, thanks to the upcoming charity match—I say goodbye to my students and my team of budding cricketers. I won't see them again for at least six weeks. Maybe I've grown sort of fond of those girls. I met them five days ago, yet they've taken to the game as if they'd received professional training. I couldn't be prouder of them for their hard work and dedication.

Does the fact that they seem to think I'm "cute" and "pretty" encourage them to work harder? Maybe. I still think it's odd that young girls apparently have crushes on me. The fact that it happens with every new group of potential cricketers doesn't make me feel any better about it.

Six weeks away from Plitherington sounds good. Except for the fact that I'm heading straight to ex-cricketer boot camp.

My mobile rings while I'm driving down the road, headed home. I answer without checking the caller ID. "Hello?"

"It's me, Dom," Chelsea says. "I need a favor."

The one hand I have on the wheel slips, and I veer into the other lane. Luckily, there's no one else in the vicinity. I clear my throat as I ease back into my lane. "You need…what?"

"A favor. That's our deal. Or are you having second thoughts about that?"

"Well, ah…no." I try to ignore the fact that my cock is rousing and it loves what she suggested. "I'm in my car right now."

"Hmm. We've already done it in your car. I'm sure we can think of something more exciting and different."

"Such as what?"

Chelsea hums, but not any particular tune, which is something she often does while thinking. "Outdoors could be fun."

"Ah, we might get arrested for that."

"Not if we choose the location carefully." Her voice drops to a sultry purr. "Doesn't the idea of screwing out in the open make you so hot?"

Yes, it does. But I've never shagged a woman outdoors or in any sort of public area. I shouldn't want to do that, but her tone of voice affected my cock almost as much as if she were here stroking it. Maybe I need a favor too. A week of coaching girls who had never touched a cricket bat before turned out to be rather stressful.

I flip through my mental catalog of places where we might shag until I find the right one. "Meet me at Richmond Park."

"Where is that?"

"Your mobile can show you the way. Stay in the car park, and I'll find you."

"Okay. See you soon."

Not many cars are there when I arrive at Richmond Park. I've only visited this place twice in my life. But I still remember how beautiful the park is, and I suppose that's why I thought of it when Chelsea suggested having sex outdoors. Something about our "favors" agreement seems to have turned me into a shamelessly randy lunatic. Public sex? I've never done that.

But when I think about public sex with Chelsea… Oh yeah, I want that.

I get out of my car and lean against it while I wait for Chelsea. Five minutes later, I see a vehicle pull into the car park. I think that's the car she hired. I'd only seen it once, so I can't be sure. But then Chelsea climbs out and waves at me while grinning. Though I push away from my car, about to trot over to her, she races over here first.

She glances around. "Wow, this is a gorgeous park. Have you been here before?"

"Only twice, when I was a boy." I wave toward the trees. "We might see wildlife in there. Shall we, ah, search for a good spot?"

"Absolutely." She smiles as we stroll toward the Capital Ring trail, her gaze drawn to a stand of trees up ahead. "Did you know that parking lot is called Spankers Hill?"

"Spankers Hill Wood, actually."

Chelsea puckers her lips, and the laughter she's desperately trying to squelch makes her splutter and hiccup. "What sort of perv decided to name that location Spankers Hill Wood?"

"A wood is a forest, you filthy-minded girl."

"Oh, come on. You must think that name sounds like a dirty joke." She bumps her shoulder into me. "Whose 'wood' got spanked out here, huh?"

"I have no idea what you're on about. I'm too innocent to understand such talk."

"Sure you are. The man who stripped naked in my studio and made me come on my desk has no idea how raunchy the name of that parking lot sounds."

I cluck my tongue. "Get your mind out of the gutter."

"You seem to have forgotten the whole purpose of this trip to the park."

"Let's walk for a bit, then talk about where to shag."

"Okay. It would be nice to take a relaxing stroll in the outdoors. This week has been a whirlwind."

I can't deny that. We've both suffered from work-related stress, and it is lovely to get outdoors and enjoy nature. We don't speak, just ambling down the path in silence while the sounds of birds and leaves rustling lull us into a companionable silence. When we reach the intersection at Pen Ponds, Chelsea wants to stop and sit down along the shore, just to appreciate the scenery.

My gaze lifts to the sky. "The sun will be setting soon."

"Already? Doesn't seem like it's late enough, but I guess I'm not used to the UK yet."

"Do you still want to shag?"

She closes her eyes, and her lips form a sweetly contented smile. "Kind of lost interest. Sorry."

"Don't apologize. I'm feeling less than enthused too."

"It's been quite a week. I'd love to just go home and go to sleep."

"You need to eat dinner, pet."

She stretches her arms above her head and sighs. "I'll probably eat the rest of that icebox cake you left for me."

"That's dessert, not dinner. Do I have to cook for you every night so you'll eat a proper meal?"

"Maybe." She leans toward me. "Watching a man cook for me is very hot."

I guide us back to the car park, but as Chelsea starts to climb into her vehicle, I lay a hand on her arm to stop her. "You are exhausted. Come to my house. I'll feed you, then you can stay the night. I'll sleep on the sofa, so you can have the bed."

"What about my car? I can't abandon it here."

I consider the problem for a moment. "Call the car hire agency and ask them to pick it up for you."

"Not sure that place is still open. Or if they'll retrieve the car for me."

"Give it a go."

She roots about in her purse until she finds the packet from the agency. Then she dials their number. Her eyes flare wide. "Are you still open? Oh, great. I, um, was hoping someone could pick up the car I rented. I don't need it anymore. Can you please do that?" She grins. "That's great. Thank you so much."

She drops her mobile into her purse. "They asked me to stay put until their guy gets here."

"Let's wait in my car."

We listen to music on the radio while we wait, and Chelsea grows sleepy. I do too. It seems like our plan to shag tonight has evaporated, and I don't mind at all. Spending time with Chelsea is enough for me. When the chap from the agency arrives only fifteen minutes later, Chelsea hands over the keys, and we leave in my car.

By the time we walk into my house, she's yawning.

"Stay awake a little longer," I say. "You need nourishment first. After all, we are leaving for Sommerleigh in the morning."

Chelsea stops dead halfway to the sofa and rotates her head to stare at me. "I completely forgot about that."

"Yes, I gathered as much." I toss my jacket onto the kitchen's bar. "Since we'll be walking into a hornet's nest of meddling and cricket rubbish, we'll both need a good night's sleep."

"Hornet's nest?" She sinks onto the sofa and sets her feet on the coffee table. "They're our friends, not a horde of angry insects."

"Sometimes it's hard to distinguish the two."

"Promise me you won't get grumpy tomorrow. Or anytime after that."

I rub my chin. "Hmm, not sure I can reasonably promise that."

"Try, Dom." She turns halfway toward me, hitting me with a sarcastically stern look. "If you can handle smitten schoolgirls, you can deal with our well-meaning friends. Chill out and enjoy our vacation in the countryside."

She's right, as much as I hate to admit it. I'd rather grouse and grumble and complain. When did I become a whingeing arse? I have a job I love, a family I love, and mates who only want to help—even if their "help" seems like interference to me. I should take Chelsea's advice and "chill out."

After dinner, I order Chelsea to go to bed. She's been yawning for half an hour, and her lids keep fluttering closed. She forces herself to stay awake by jerking her drooping head up and rubbing her eyes. I finally take matters into my own hands and pluck her off the sofa, carrying her into the bedroom. I pull the covers back and toss her onto the mattress.

Chelsea props herself up on her elbows. "I can't sleep in my clothes again."

"Feel free to undress."

She starts to pull her shirt up.

I throw a hand up. "Not in front of me."

"Why not? We've had sex twice already." She gets a sly look on her face. "Besides, I've seen you stark naked, but you haven't seen all of me."

"Let's leave that for another time." I march over to the closet and retrieve a shirt for her. Since I grabbed the first thing I saw, it turned out to be my cricket shirt. I toss it to her. "Wear this."

"Suddenly shy about nudity?" She slips my shirt on over her clothes, then begins to shimmy out of her blouse and bra without removing the shirt. She does the same with her trousers. "Happy now?"

"Yes, thank you." I walk over to the doorway, then glance back. "Good night, Chelsea."

"Night, Dominic," she says while yawning.

That's adorable, and I want to rush over there to kiss her. Instead, I shut the door and settle in on the sofa for the night. When I wake up in the morning, I'm pleasantly surprised to discover I haven't gotten a crick in every muscle in my body. The sofa isn't sized for a man of my height, after all. Why do I need a large piece of furniture? I live alone.

But not last night. I had a woman in my bed. Sure, Chelsea was in my bedroom—but with a closed door between us and her snores echoing through the house. Strangely, even her snoring seems adorable to me.

I've walked halfway to the bedroom, on my way there to shout for Chelsea to get up, when my mobile rings. I jog back to the living room and hunt about until I remember where I left my mobile. Then I fumble to answer it.

"Eat light this morning," Hugh Parrish announces. "We're having a big brunch at ten thirty."

"Pardon?"

"You heard me, Dominic. Pick up Chelsea and head straight to Sommerleigh. If you must eat, keep it light. We've organized a lavish brunch to kick off the festivities."

"I thought this little holiday was strictly so all of us retired cricketers could practice on the huge lawn at Sommerleigh."

"Do as I said, no questions. Lord Sommerleigh commands it."

The arse hangs up on me. What choice do I have? I race to the bedroom and bang my fist on the door. "Wake up, Chelsea."

"Let me sleep in, please."

"Can't. Lord Sommerleigh has decreed that we must attend brunch at his estate."

And the meddling is about to begin.

Chapter Fourteen

Chelsea

I yawn loudly, rubbing my eyes to try to clear the sleep from them and to wake myself up. Last night, I slept better than I have in a long time. Something about sleeping in Dominic's bed acted like a sedative, and I conked out within a few minutes, not rousing again until he started banging on the door. I'd spent the night surrounded by the scent of Dominic, a smell I can't describe, though it makes me feel like I'm wrapped up in his body.

That's dumb. I'm drowsy, which makes my brain fuzzy, and that's the only reason I'm thinking about how good Dominic smells.

But he does smell good. Always.

The man in question bangs on the door again. "Wake up, Chelsea, or I'm coming in to drag you out of bed."

"Okay, okay." I yawn again, just as loudly as before, and swing my legs over the side of the bed. When my soles touch the cold wood floor, I shiver. "What did you do with my clothes, Dom?"

"They're in the drawer of the nightstand."

I pull out the drawer and snatch up my clothes. "No more banging and no barging in either. I'm getting dressed."

"Finally. I'll wait out here."

"Go into the living room."

"Oh, no. I'm not leaving this spot until you open the door. Don't trust you not to fall asleep again."

Ugh. He is so stubborn. That might be kind of hot, but it's also very annoying right now. Once I'm dressed, I fling the door open. "I'm awake and fully clothed. Happy now, Mr. Bossy Pants?"

"Yes. I'm deliriously happy."

"No need to go insane over it." I plant a hand on his chest and push, but he doesn't budge. "Move your bloomin' arse."

"That was a horrible attempt at a British accent. Would you like me to tutor you in how we actually speak?"

"No thank you. I need food, not a lecture."

He wags a finger in my face. "A light snack only. We are expected at Sommerleigh for brunch."

I roll my eyes and huff. "When is that? I'm starving."

"For what?" He grasps my hips and tugs me into his body. "Food or a favor?"

"Thought we were in a big hurry. I can eat a granola bar in one minute flat, but a favor takes longer."

"You do want one, then. Instead of a granola bar."

I wish he wouldn't speak in that deep, hungry tone. It makes my clib throb and my nipples stiffen, which in turn causes them to scrape against my bra. Can't forget about his erection either. It rubs against my belly.

Oh God, do I ever need a favor.

Dom slides his hands down to my ass. "I excel at quickies. Let's take the edge off together."

I want to say yes, but I should tell him no. My brain seems to have stalled, unable to choose an option. Screw or eat, eat or screw. Screw or eat, eat or screw. "Yes, okay, yes. But no dawdling."

He salutes. "Yes, my queen."

"Oh, please. You're overdoing it."

"How about we fuck on the bar?"

"Fine. Just do it already."

Dominic chuckles. "I love the way you get so impatient when we're about to shag."

He picks me up and strides into the living room.

The doorbell rings.

I moan pitifully. "Who is that? You promised to fuck me."

Dominic sets me down and marches to the door, flinging it open. "Derek? What are you doing here? I thought you were at Sommerleigh. Then again, you are American, so maybe you got lost on the streets of London."

"Nope. I'm exactly where I need to be."

I trot over there to stand beside Dominic. But I look at Derek. "Why are you dressed like a secret service agent?"

"Because I'm a bodyguard."

"Yeah, I know. But you don't have anyone to guard."

"Sure I do." He glances sideways and nods, then crooks one finger. "Come over here, Ms. Sangster. Chelsea thinks you don't exist."

Diana Sangster, the billionaire businesswoman, steps into view. "You should get used to calling me Mrs. Hahn, darling. We will be married in two months."

"I've got better names I want to call you, but only in private."

"Are you lot done flirting?" Dominic asks. "Maybe you should tell us why you're here."

"We're the escort," Derek says. "Lord Sticky ordered us to 'retrieve the wayward couple,' and you know I always do what he says."

I look at Dom. "Lord Sticky?"

"That's the nickname Derek gave to Hugh."

Derek smirks. "He hates it. That's why I keep calling him Lord Sticky. Guess you didn't hear that during Hugh and Avery's wedding week extravaganza."

"Guess not," I say. "That's all very fascinating, but Dominic and I have something to take care of first. You go ahead to Sommerleigh, and we'll follow in Dom's car later."

"Uh-uh-uh." Derek wags a finger at me. "I am under strict orders to abduct—uh, strenuously invite you to come with us now. Resistance is futile."

I turn toward Dominic, but he only shrugs.

"We've got snacks in the limo," Derek says. "You won't starve, and we'll make sure to keep you occupied so the two and half hour drive will fly by."

Doesn't it just figure? I wanted a snack, but Dom talked me into sex instead. Now I have to settle for food, when what I really want now is for Dom to screw me.

I dutifully grab my purse, and Dominic and I follow our captors out of the building to a waiting limo. At least we get to travel in style. Once we've slid onto the butter-soft leather benches that face each other, I finally succumb to the inevitable. No favor today. It shouldn't bother me so much that we can't have sex. I mean, this favor arrangement was supposed to be strictly for stress relief. I'm not stressed. I'm plain old horny.

Derek and Diana do make the long drive to Sommerleigh fly by, mostly because they regale us with jokes and lots of stories about the wacky antics of Dominic's British buddies. I love hearing about how Derek the bodyguard fell for his client, Diana the business tycoon, despite their nine-year age difference. I hadn't visited the UK for a while, until Hugh and Avery brought me here under the guise of the charity event. I did meet Derek and Diana at Lord Sommerleigh's wedding, but I only talked to them briefly.

Now, I'll get to spend more time around Dom's friends.

I'd been to Sommerleigh once before, and I can't wait to spend more time at the estate that's been home to the Parrishes for generations.

Finally, we turn off the road and roll down the long, tree-shrouded driveway that leads to the house. Just when I think we've gotten lost in the woods, the trees part to reveal the circular driveway and the large open area that surrounds the manor. Sommerleigh House is a somewhat boxy structure, but it has all the regal charm Americans like me expect from a British aristocrat's home. The title of Viscount Sommerleigh has been passed down through the generations.

The current Lord Sommerleigh jumps out of the limo the second it rolls to a stop at the foot of the house's steps. Hugh offers his hand to his wife. "Lady Sommerleigh, may I assist you?"

"Thank you, Lord Sommerleigh."

I glance at Dominic with my brows raised. He shrugs. Guess he doesn't understand the way Avery and Hugh talk to each other either. Sometimes she calls her husband Lord Steamy, his unofficial and naughty secondary title. Other times, they refer to each other by their official titles. It seems kind of weird to me when they call each other lord and lady. But then, I'm not British.

Dominic seems confused by it too. So maybe it's not only Americans who think the whole aristocrat thing is bizarre.

As soon as Avery has exited the limo, Dominic leaps out to offer me his hand. I take it, though I don't actually need help getting out of the car. I assume he's offering me his hand so I won't feel slighted in the face of Hugh's chivalry toward his wife. Dom knows me better than that, though. I appreciate it if a man offers me his hand, but I don't care if he doesn't.

"Thank you, Dominic," I say as I step out of the limo.

"If you think I'm a ruddy moron, you can just say so."

"Why would I think that? Your gesture was very sweet."

He shuts the car door. "Some women don't want a man to treat them like, ah…"

"A lady? Come on, you know I'm not sensitive about that." I kiss his cheek. "You can offer me your hand anytime."

His lips tick up at the corners. "I can think of several ways I could offer you my hand, and they're all filthy."

"Try to behave yourself. We don't want anyone to figure out we're, um, doing each other favors."

"Of course. I know how to be discreet."

"Are you guys coming?" Avery calls out to us. She and Hugh are standing at the top of the steps.

She has no idea what a loaded question that is. We're not coming yet, but maybe we will later.

We follow Hugh and Avery into the house, and their butler, Kendall, greets us. He looks like a young man but has the composure of someone much older. Kendall always calls Hugh "sir." On the other occasions when I visited Sommerleigh, Hugh winced every time Kendall called him "sir," but these days, he has finally accepted the butler's deference. I suppose becoming a married man changed his outlook.

"May I escort your guests to their rooms, sir?" Kendall asks Hugh.

"That won't be necessary." Hugh turns to me and Dominic. "Your rooms are upstairs. Avery and I will show you."

We follow Lord and Lady Sommerleigh up the wide staircase to the second floor and down the hallway.

"Here we are," Hugh says. "Dominic, your room is on the left. Chelsea yours is on the right."

We are standing between two doorways. Sommerleigh is a huge house with enough rooms for all the Parrishes' British buddies. Did the lord and lady of the manor put Dom and me in adjacent rooms on purpose? I'd bet my left kidney they did. It's part of their meddling plan.

Dominic squints at Hugh, then swings the nearest door open so he can peer inside. He aims a hard, squinty stare at Lord Sommerleigh. "Adjoining rooms?"

Hugh feigns innocence better than anyone I've ever met. "The other rooms are already taken. You should have come earlier. The other cricketers claimed their rooms yesterday."

"You told us to arrive today. We rode in your limousine."

I glance back and forth between Dominic and Hugh. "What's the big deal about adjoining rooms? There's a door between them."

"With a lock on it," Hugh says. "If Dom is terrified you might sneak into his room, he can simply lock the door."

Yeah, our time at Sommerleigh will be full of sarcasm and ribbing. I might need to slip a tranquilizer into Dominic's food.

Chapter Fifteen

Dominic

I'm not terrified, you sodding arse," I say, though my tone is
more mocking then angry. I'm well-acquainted with my mates'
tendency to interfere in other people's lives. "I knew you'd be
meddling, but I thought you'd wait at least an hour before you
started in on that rubbish."

Hugh claps a hand on my shoulder. "Try to enjoy yourself. This
is an extended holiday for you and Chelsea."

I narrow my gaze on him. "Holiday? I thought this was boot
camp for aged former cricketers."

"That too. But we've scheduled plenty of downtime for you lot to
rest and enjoy yourselves."

I point at the doorway behind me. "Which room is mine?"

"Whichever you like. This one is slightly larger than the adjacent
room."

Though I want to chastise the arse for his interfering ways, I
barely manage to open my mouth before Chelsea intervenes.

"We're fine with the arrangements you've made, Hugh," she
says. "Why don't you and Avery go downstairs? Dom and I can
get settled in on our own. And thank you so much for invit-
ing me to stay at Sommerleigh too. You guys have a beautiful
home."

Lord and Lady Sommerleigh say goodbye and disappear down the staircase.

Chelsea turns to me. "Should we toss a coin?"

"For what?"

"Deciding who gets which room."

"There's nothing to decide. You will take the larger one." I nod toward the doorway. "Go on. Kendall will bring our bags up."

I stand here watching while she walks into her room and shuts the door. My entire body feels as if someone has inserted a live electrical wire up my arse and the current crackles down my nerves. Why am I so anxious? I used to play cricket for a living, but now the thought of even playing a private match makes me tense.

Why am I still staring at the closed door to Chelsea's room?

I give myself a mental slap and trudge to the door of the other room. It's larger than one person needs, but I won't complain about that. Avery and Hugh are doing a wonderful thing, setting up this charity event, though I wish they hadn't inserted meddling into the mix. Still, I know they honestly want to raise money for cancer research, and I want to help them do that.

Not sure if watching aged cricketers flounder on the field will draw in donations.

After Kendall drops off my bags, I knock on the door that connects my suite to Chelsea's.

She smiles when she opens the door. "Miss me already? Or do you need help unpacking?"

"Neither. I wondered if you know how we're meant to dress for brunch."

"With clothes on, I assume. I know some of your friends went to a nudist resort a few years ago, but this is a stately British manor."

"I meant what sort of clothes. Casual, formal, something in between."

She shrugs. "Nobody told me anything about that."

"Hmm. Guess I should ring Hugh."

"Or you could walk down the stairs to ask him in person."

I lean against the doorjamb. "Isn't that passé these days? No one speaks in person unless their mobile dies."

"That's cute, but you could have gone downstairs to ask Hugh in the time it took you to make sarcastic comments about modern life."

She does make a good point.

I pull my mobile out of my trouser pocket and dial Hugh's number. "What is the dress code for today's brunch, Lord Sommerleigh?"

"Dress code? An adult should know how to clothe himself."

"Why can't you ever answer a question like a normal person?"

"That is so bourgeois. But if you insist on a dull response, the dress code is business casual. Satisfied?"

No, I'm not. But at least I have an idea of what sort of clothes to wear. "Why is it business casual? We aren't conducting negotiations."

Hugh blows out a frustrated sigh. "Dress how you bloody well like. But please shag Chelsea first so the rest of us won't have to listen to you grousing."

"I am not—" I almost blurted out that I'm not shagging Chelsea, but that isn't true. Well, I'm not fucking her right this minute. But I might do later. "Sorry. I guess I'm a bit anxious about cricket boot camp."

"No worries. I was once abducted by a mob of angry Scots and held hostage in their castle. Your outburst didn't bother me at all. Come downstairs whenever you're ready." His tone turns devious. "Or perhaps you'd rather come upstairs."

"Piss off, Hugh."

I disconnect the call.

Chelsea taps a finger on my lips. "You look like you need a favor."

"Not now. Hugh told me to shag you, but I refuse to give him the satisfaction of being right about that."

"So instead, you'll act like a grumpy bear." She lays her hands on my chest, and her body hovers millimeters from mine. "Let me do you a quick favor, so you'll be relaxed at brunch."

"We don't have time."

"Sure we do." Chelsea drops to her knees, which places her head directly in front of my groin. Then she reaches for the zipper on my trousers. "You need some stress relief."

My cock loves the idea, but for reasons I can't explain, I don't want her to do that. Not right now. So I grasp her shoulders and urge her to stand up. "I will be fine. Change into something business casual and meet me in the hall."

"Don't think I have anything like that in my suitcase."

"Hugh told me the dress code is business casual, but I think he was having me on."

"Okay. I'll wear whatever, then."

She shuts the door.

And I change clothes while my cock keeps threatening to give me a hard-on. I fill my mind with thoughts of playing cricket for the first time in years, and that does the trick. My cock deflates like a leaky balloon. I love cricket, but I suppose I am feeling uncertain about these events Hugh and Avery have arranged. It's not as if we'll play the charity match in a huge stadium. I'm sure it will be a smaller venue with a sparse crowd. Most people will donate their money without attending the match.

Chelsea and I walk downstairs together. She looks lovely as always, wearing a casual dress that flatters her figure. She did something with her hair too, something that makes it seem fluffier and shinier or…I don't know. She looks lovely, that's all.

This pang in my chest has nothing to do with her clothing or her hairstyle. It's nothing but a meaningless, fleeting sensation.

We enter the dining room to find a crowd of people waiting for us. I greet Hugh, Avery, and Hugh's mother, Rosalyn. The other has-been cricketers are here too, but I'm not sure how to greet them. I'd never met these blokes during my pro days, though I knew of them. Don't think I ever played a match against any of them, and I definitely never played on the same team.

Once Chelsea and I have taken our seats, Hugh rises. "It's time to meet your teammates, Dominic." He points to each bloke as he announces their names, and I nod to every man. "Chip Martel. Benno Hochberg. Colton Ward. Gilbert Paquet. Mickey Randall. Declan O'Hara. Glen Roydon. Will Banks. Brian Wortham. Terry Cash."

"Good to meet you," I say. "I'm sure our little match will raise a bit of money for a good cause."

"A bit?" Hugh gives me what seems like a look of genuine surprise. "No, no, no. Our goal is to raise five million pounds, at least."

"From one little cricket match?"

"Why do you persist in calling it a 'little' match?" Hugh sets his hands on the table and stares at me. "This event will draw international attention. My darling wife will make certain of that. Avery is more than just an image consultant, after all. She is also a talented and well-respected publicist who has already arranged the media blitz for our event."

International? Media blitz? No one warned me about any of that.

Chelsea settles a hand on my arm. "Are you okay, Dom? You look pale all of a sudden."

I'm fairly certain I have indeed gone pale. I'm also positive that my mouth is gaping and my eyes are wide.

"What's wrong with you, Dom?" Hugh asks. "If you're about to be sick, I should ring for Kendall to bring a bucket."

"I am not about to vomit." While everyone gawps at me, I take two slow, deep breaths. But I don't feel calmer until Chelsea grasps my hand under the table. "You should have told me this would be a huge event, Hugh. I've been blindsided."

Chip Martel shakes his head at me. "Loosen up, mate. It's all for fun and a good cause. Think of how much money the calendar will bring in for cancer research—and how many girls will salivate over us."

I slouch in my chair. "Can we just eat now and stop talking about the big event? I'm famished."

"Of course," Hugh says. "Let's eat."

The brunch offers plenty of delicious foods, and I consume far more than I should. Stress eating, I suppose. Maybe I should have taken Chelsea up on her offer to do me a favor by sucking me off. Too late now. She's having fun chatting to the other cricketers, who make her laugh with their bawdy jokes and humorous tales of life on the pro cricketing circuit. Rosalyn Parrish has been seated beside me, so I talk to her throughout the meal.

When Declan O'Hara makes a casual pass at Chelsea, I feel my entire body tensing up and my hands balling into fists. What in the world is wrong with me? I don't get jealous. I never used to care if some other bloke made a pass at Chelsea. But now, I want to batter that Irish arsehole.

Chelsea squeezes my hand under the table as she leans in to murmur, "Are you okay?"

"Yes, fine," I whisper. "You should tell that Irish wanker to leave off."

"I guess you mean Declan. What's your problem with him? He's a nice guy."

"He's been trying it on with you."

She snorts, as if she needed to work hard not to laugh at me. "Not every man wants to get in my pants."

"All of these wankers do."

Chelsea studies me for a moment, then curls her lips into a knowing smile. "I think I get it."

"What?"

"You're jealous."

Now I snort, though with derision, not repressed laughter. "That's ridiculous."

"I don't think so. You never cared if men flirted with me." She squeezes my thigh. "Not until we started doing you-know-what."

We're both still whispering, so I can't imagine why she felt the need to say "you-know-what" instead of the word shag or fuck or any number of other descriptive terms for our favors. In fact, she could have used the word favor.

"Let's not discuss this here," I say. "Our mates are starting to stare at us."

Hugh rises and clears his throat. "Brunch has been lovely, but it's time for the cricketers to have their first team meeting."

"You're wanting us to play immediately after eating?" I say. "We'll get cramps or something. And we'll be bloody awful on the field when we have full stomachs."

"This is a meeting only. No practice yet. We'll start that to-morrow."

Wonderful. I'll have an entire day to get more anxious about the massive international blitz that will surround our charity match and that sodding calendar.

When Chelsea and I say goodbye in the hall, she raises onto her tiptoes to whisper, "Try to have a good time. Your teammates are good people, not the enemy."

"No, Hugh Parrish is my nemesis. I'm plotting the best way to murder him and get away with it."

She kisses my cheek. "Be nice, Dom."

I lower my voice to barely a murmur. "I will be needing a favor after this meeting."

"Yeah, I figured. Think I'll need that too, since Avery and I will be rummaging through all the shots I've taken of you guys so far."

Avery calls out to Chelsea from the other end of the hall, and the two women disappear into the solarium. That room does have the best lighting, with all those enormous glass windows, and ought to provide the perfect place to go over all those pictures.

Only now do I realize what Chelsea said. *All the shots I've taken of you guys so far.*

I groan. She wants more photos. *Bugger me.*

Chapter Sixteen

Chelsea

Dominic seemed stressed out when I left him in the downstairs hall. Did he figure out that I'm going to take more shots of the cricketers? I probably shouldn't have mentioned that I'll be going over the photos I have "so far." Dominic is too smart not to notice that, unless he's so anxious that my statement flew right over his head.

Avery and I spend an hour poring over the shots. We both love all the photographs, and we could easily go with the ones I'd taken during the week. But we agree that we would really love to try some outdoor shots too. That means asking the men to pose for me again. Only one man might balk at the prospect of going in front of the camera one more time.

Yeah, his name is Dominic Rigby.

I march out to the big lawn behind the house, where I can see the cricketers gathered there. They aren't wearing uniforms. They don't seem to be practicing either. I guess they're discussing things, though I can't even guess what a conversation about a cricket match would involve if it's not training or strategy.

Benno Hochberg spots me approaching, though the others seem too deep in conversation to notice. The German flirt grins and whoops. "The entertainment is here! Who ordered a stripper?"

Dominic's head swivels in my direction, and his neutral expression twists into a scowl. "Shut your bloody mouth, Hochberg. You know Chelsea is not a stripper."

"It was a joke, Rigby. Chelsea isn't offended, are you?"

"Nope, not at all." I halt beside Dominic. "It's nice to see you cricket hunks again. And I'm glad you're all here. I'll only need to make my announcement once instead of twelve times."

Dominic's brows hike up. "Announcement? About what?"

"You'll find out in sec." I shove two fingers into my mouth and blow, emitting an ear-splitting whistle. When everyone stops talking, and they focus on me, I continue. "Avery and I agreed that we would really like to have more shots of all you guys. The studio ones are great, but we want to experiment with some other options to make sure we get the absolute best images for the calendar."

"More shots?" Dominic says with all the enthusiasm of someone who just got the news that his cocker spaniel died. "I thought we were done with that rubbish."

"Nope. More rubbish is coming your way." I thump my fist into his bicep. Never noticed before how thick and powerful his arm muscles are. "Are you going to help with this project? Or do I need to get Derek out here to pummel you into submission?"

"Did I suggest I wouldn't do my part? I may not enjoy it, but I would never say no to you."

Chip Martel jogs up to me. "Don't worry about him, lovey. You've got me, and I'll pose for you as many times you want." He winks. "Maybe you'll pose for me too."

"No, she will not," Dominic virtually snarls. "Keep your ruddy hands off Chelsea. She's doing a job, not providing brothel services to randy cricketers."

"Stop it, Dom," I say. "You're overreacting."

And since when does he care if other men flirt with me? Chip and Benno aren't serious. They're just having fun. Dominic has behaved strangely ever since he found out about the calendar, and I will figure out why, one way or another. But first, I need to schedule the shoots for the additional photos I want to gather.

Dominic watches while each cricketer comes up to me and chooses a slot on the schedule I'd created on my phone. None of them really care which slot they get. Even Dominic doesn't grouse about it.

"The last one is yours," I tell him. "You could've had your choice if you'd come over here first. Instead, you let the others grab all the best slots on my schedule."

"I have the perfect slot."

"But it's the last one of the day—at six pm."

"And that is perfect for me. All those other chancers will be busy playing poker and drinking." He curls a lock of my hair around his finger. "I can have you for as long as I like."

"You've got that backwards. I'll have you, since I'm the photographer and the one in charge of the calendar."

"But you can have me whenever you like."

I already know that. And the sensual tone of his voice is turning me on.

"Dinner!" Hugh shouts. "Get your arses in gear. Everyone is waiting on you two."

We trot into the house to join the others in the dining room. After the main course, dessert is served. But Dom and I make our excuses, claiming we're too full for dessert, and sneak back upstairs. On the landing, Dominic stops us.

"Go into your room," he says. "I have a wicked idea."

"You want a favor."

"Do I ever."

"But you said no beds."

Dominic's mouth curves into a suggestive smile that's sexy as hell and laced with simmering heat. "Who said anything about using the bed? Go into your room, pet, and wait for my call."

I hurry inside and shut the door. My pulse had sped up the second he declared that he had a wicked idea, and by the time I'd shut the door, I was already slick and achy in all the best places. Whatever Dom wants to do tonight, I'm ready for it. So ready.

My cell phone rings. I swipe to take the call, but I don't get the chance to say hello. He speaks first.

"You have a full-length mirror, correct?"

"That's right."

"Strip down to your bra and knickers, then kneel in front of the mirror, facing it so you can see yourself."

"Okay." I follow his instructions, now kneeling before the mirror, gazing at my own reflection. My nipples jut out beneath the fabric of my bra, and a few hairs poke out from under my skimpy panties. "What's next?"

"Run your hands over your entire body. Feel every dip and swell, the curve of your lush breasts, the firmness of your nipples, everything. And tell me how it makes you feel."

While I slide my hands over my own body, I swear I can feel Dom's hands on my skin as if he were behind me, guiding my fingers. "Oh God, this is incredible. I'm getting even more turned on, like I could almost come."

"Not yet, love. Push your hands inside your knickers, over your buttocks, and massage your arse."

I do that too while my pulse quickens and my breaths become heavier. "I love how this feels. Makes me imagine you touching me there."

A fleeting thought rushes through me—is this still a quick favor?—but the notion evaporates quickly. All I can think about is following Dom's commands because I've never experienced anything this erotic before.

"Now slide your hands around to the front and stroke your mound." His voice has gotten rougher and sexier, so much so that my breath hitches. "Are you doing that, Chelsea?"

"Yes. Mm, I'm so wet for you."

"Exactly how I want you, darling."

"Tell me what to do now. Please."

He chuckles, the sound deep and throaty. "Excited, aren't you? Push a finger between your folds and stroke your clit."

I gasp as I fulfill his command. My clit is so rigid and slick, and I want to rub myself to orgasm. But not until Dom tells me to do that. "I need to come, please, I'll go crazy if I can't finish this."

"Uh-uh-uh. Get rid of your bra and knickers."

"Hold on. I need to set my phone down." I switch on the speaker, then toss the phone onto the bed and strip off my underwear. "Okay, I did that."

"If you moved away from the mirror, go back over there."

"Give me a sec." I hurry back into position. "I'm ready."

"Fold your arms over your chest, then close your eyes. Tell me when you've done that."

"I did it."

"Now don't move a muscle."

For a moment that feels like eternity, I stand here waiting, growing more impatient every second because he got me so wound up. Then I hear the click of a door opening, followed by the sounds of someone breathing. His hands grasp my hips at the same instant that his knees nudge my calves. Or maybe that's his foot. I don't care either way.

"Open your eyes, love, and look in the mirror."

When I obey his command, the mirror shows me myself—and Dominic behind me. His big hands feel warm, and I can tell he's naked, though my body hides most of him from view. His cock brushes against my lower back.

"Are you wearing a condom?" I ask. "Your dick is slippery."

"Yes, I have a condom."

"Why?" Jeez, that was dumbest question ever.

He chuckles again, and that rough, sexy sound makes my clit throb. "Why? Because I want to fuck you, darling."

"Yes, please, I need you inside me."

"Watch us in the mirror."

He shifts position just enough that he can push his cock between my thighs, though he doesn't thrust inside me. I gasp and rock my hips back, desperate to feel his length between my folds. Dominic slides his hands over my belly, then glides one further down to cup my groin. I instinctively spread my legs a little, enough that he could push his fingers into my drenched and aching folds if he wanted.

"Keep watching the mirror, Chelsea. Keep watching us."

I fixate my gaze on the mirror, where I can see Dom's hungry expression and his fingers rubbing my folds. I raise my arms, locking my hands at his nape, and rock my hips into the movements of his fingers.

"Fuck," he groans, drawing out that one syllable. "Can't wait. You're driving me out of my mind."

I can't think or speak. The only sounds emerging from me are moans and whimpers and other embarrassingly desperate noises. But I don't mind my desperation, not when Dominic is the one doing this to me.

He grasps my hips again, pulls back, and plunges his cock inside me. I barely have time to register the change before he starts pumping into me with such vigor that my knees lift slightly off the floor with every thrust. He pumps faster and harder, making my tits bounce and his balls thwap against my ass. We watch ourselves in the mirror for the entire time, our reflected gazes bound to each other. Dom grunts and gasps, palming one breast while he shoves his fingers between my folds to mercilessly rub my clit.

I come so hard that I can't even scream. Dom keeps fucking me and rasping his finger over my nub while my body pulsates around his cock. To feel his length molded to my inner muscles, over and over, it pushes me into an even more intense climax.

Dominic pounds into me three more times, shouting like a wild beast, and sags against me. His chin rests on my shoulder. His ragged breaths bluster over my cheek. "Bloody hell. That was—"

He buries his face against my neck, as if he can't think of anything else to say.

I lay a palm on his cheek. "Yeah, it was."

Neither of us knows what to say. We agreed to quick favors, not the hottest mirror sex ever. Gazing into each other's eyes the whole time doesn't seem like a simple favor. Have we blown our arrangement apart like an atomic bomb? My orgasm was explosive, for sure.

The better question is, do I care if we blew past the line between friends with favors and honest-to-goodness lovers?

Dominic backs away from me, his cock retreating from my body, and clears his throat. "That was…different."

"Yeah." I suddenly feel anxious, but I force myself to waddle around on my knees to face him. His pinched expression is not encouraging. "Are you okay, Dom?"

"I suppose so."

Oh, shit. He's freaked out about our intensely intimate and sensual mirror sex. Why else would he seem so uncomfortable? This was his idea, but now he clearly regrets it.

I wrap my arms around myself and bite down on the inside of my lip. "Maybe you should go back to your room."

His pained expression disintegrates. "No, darling, I am not leaving this room."

Then he throws his arms around me, hugs me tight, and kisses me.

Chapter Seventeen

Dominic

Chelsea holds still while I press my lips to hers, and just when I'm starting to think I've made a terrible mistake, her whole body sags into me and she exhales a soft moan. The first time I'd kissed her, we were both, ah… not quite inebriated, but not entirely clearheaded either. Tonight, we are both stone cold sober. Drunk on lust, but in full possession of our faculties.

I crush my mouth to hers more firmly, gliding my palms down her back until my fingers graze the upper curves of her arse cheeks. She moans again and flicks her tongue between my lips, seeking permission or maybe fighting the impulse to deepen the kiss. I can't stop myself. I plunge my tongue into her mouth.

She tastes even better than the first time.

With her tits mounded against my chest, their tips rub against me every time she wriggles. But when she flings her arms around my neck, a deep groan resonates through me.

Chelsea severs the kiss first, though she keeps her body plastered to mine. She's as breathless as I am. "Wow, Dominic, that was…unexpected."

"Which part? When I fucked you in front of the mirror? Or when I kissed you?"

"All of that, plus the domineering way you talked to me on the phone."

A lock of hair has fallen over her eye, so I tuck it behind her ear. "I think we need to talk about our favors agreement."

"There's nothing to say about it."

I feel as if the floor must have collapsed down into the foyer, and any moment screams will erupt down there. But I'm still kneeling on the bedroom floor. Her statement hit me so hard that I've become incapable of moving a single muscle.

"What's wrong?" Chelsea asks. "You look like you might throw up."

"You said there's nothing to say about our favors. That sounded like you don't want to be with me anymore."

She freezes, and even her eyelids don't move. Then she bursts out laughing.

I glower at her. "If you don't want to shag me anymore, just say so. Laughing is not appropriate."

"You're adorable." She wipes tears from her eyes and takes hold of my face. "There's nothing to say because we obviously aren't doing each other favors anymore. We've moved past that into relationship territory. Wouldn't you agree?"

"I, well…" The relief that floods through me prevents me from finishing that sentence. Not that I had a clue how to respond. But I figure it out at last. "Yes, I agree."

"That's all you want to say right now?"

"No, but I can't trust myself not to blurt out something embarrassingly romantic."

She gives me a quick, firm kiss. "We're alone. You can gush all you want, and I won't make fun of you."

"You did laugh hysterically at me a moment ago."

"I didn't laugh that hard." She lashes her arms around my neck. "I'm sorry for the way I reacted. But you honestly can tell me anything. Don't you know that by now? We've been friends for nine years, and we've been lovers for almost a week. Nobody knows me better than you do."

"And you know me just as thoroughly. But where do we go from here?"

"We've got two choices." She squints as if she's thinking hard. "It's a tough decision. Your bed or mine?"

I study her bed. And I pretend to be horrified. "Yours is bigger than mine. How is that fair? I'm twice your size, but Lord and Lady Sommerleigh gave you the largest bed."

"You aren't twice my size." She moves onto the foot of the bed with her legs dangling off the end and swings her feet. "Male models are always such prima donnas."

"I am not a model."

"Sorry to burst your bubble, but you posed for professional photographs. That means you are a model."

"Don't ever call me that again." I pick her up and toss her onto the center of the mattress. "I am The Dom, remember? I dominate the cricket field and you."

"Only when we're having sex."

I pretend that I'm considering the issue. "Maybe we should shag on the pitch. Then you could have both sides of me—the cricket Dom and the sex Dom."

"That would mean public sex."

"Not if we do it at night, after everyone else has gone to sleep."

"I like the way you think." Chelsea's mouth gapes open on a loud yawn. "Not tonight, though."

"We can wait." I pull the covers back, and we cuddle up together under the sheets. "Should we tell our friends about our new status?"

"Uh-huh. But in the morning. Sleep with me now, please."

"Anything for you, love."

I can't say which one of us falls asleep first because I don't even realize it happened. The next thing I know, I'm opening my eyes and the sun is beaming through the big windows. Chelsea lies pressed against my front side with her arse nestled against my groin. I don't recall rolling over, and I somehow didn't notice when she turned over to spoon with me. Don't care how it happened. I love waking up with her warm, supple body cradled against me.

She doesn't rouse even when my cock begins to wake up and slowly stiffens into a morning erection. Her lips are curled into the sweetest sleeping smile. I wonder what she's dreaming of, but I won't disturb her just so I can find out the answer. She is so beautiful, and I can't believe it took me this long to realize how much she means to me.

Yes, I am a moron.

Chelsea stirs and exhales a soft little sigh. Her lids flutter but don't quite open.

I slide my arm over her belly and tug her into me, nuzzling her hair. "Are you awake yet, love?"

She mumbles.

"Not quite conscious, hmm?" I move my hand up to cradle her tit in my palm. "Maybe I can speed up the process."

Chelsea rolls onto her back, whisking her body away from me. She wags a finger. "You are a bad influence. We both have work to do today, and you've always claimed that sex before a match will hinder your performance."

"Why did I ever say that? It's bollocks. Shagging you will give me all the energy I need to destroy my teammates."

"Aren't you supposed to support them? Destruction doesn't seem like team spirit."

"You are more important than any sport." I push up on one elbow. "This is Sunday, when most people rest and recuperate. Yet I'm required to train. Won't we all be smited for that?"

"I think it's smote, not smited."

"Whatever."

Someone bangs on the door. Hugh shouts, "Time to rise and shine. Finish your shagging and get dressed. Breakfast will be served in eighteen minutes, according to Kendall."

I glance at Chelsea, and she wrinkles her brows. Since she clearly doesn't understand my dilemma, I whisper, "He's waiting for a response, and if I answer, he'll know we're a couple."

"So what?"

"We haven't announced that development yet."

Chelsea rolls her eyes.

And Hugh shouts, "Are you alive in there? Or have you both suffered heart attacks from relentlessly shagging?"

My girlfriend sits up and hollers, "I'm alone in here, Lord Sommerleigh. But I'll make sure Dominic wakes up too."

"I see." Hugh's tone has become far too self-satisfied. "Do let Chelsea 'wake you up,' Dominic. Everyone is waiting for you two in the dining room."

His footsteps fade away, so at least he finally buggered off.

Chelsea watches me while I hop off the bed. But she seizes my hand when I move toward the door to my room. "Why didn't you want to tell Hugh about us? He knows you were in here with me."

"We haven't announced our—"

"That's bullshit. Tell me the real reason."

I wince and scratch the back of my neck. "Maybe I feel like a bloody fool for not realizing sooner that you're more to me than a friend. It took me nine years."

"Took me that long too."

"We're a pair of ruddy fools, aren't we?"

"Damn idiots, I'd say."

I suppose knowing each other for so long made it more difficult for us to come to terms with our real feelings. I should have known a week ago, shouldn't I? Every time Chelsea had another photo shoot with the other cricketers, I got jealous.

"We've both been blind," I say, "but now our eyes are wide open."

"So, what do we do now?"

"Have breakfast with our mates." I jump off the bed and start walking toward the door.

"Wrong way, Dom. Unless you want to announce to our friends that you've become a nudist."

My hand is curled around the knob, and I suddenly realize I'm about to open the door to the hallway, not the one that adjoins her bedroom. "Sorry. I wasn't paying attention."

Chelsea laughs at me. "Get dressed. We'll announce our new relationship status over breakfast. I guarantee no one will be surprised."

"No, they wouldn't be."

I leave the adjoining door open while we both pull on some clothes, though I have no idea how aristocrats dress for breakfast. They'll have to accept that I wear jeans and a T-shirt. Chelsea chooses a lovely casual outfit consisting of pale blue trousers and a long white shirt that hangs below her hips. I don't care what she wears. She's beautiful in anything—or nothing at all.

We amble into the dining room one minute before Hugh's deadline.

Everyone cheers as if we've just returned from winning a great battle. My fellow cricketers join in as Hugh, Avery, and Rosalyn clap and whistle and whoop. What on earth is wrong with these people? I ignore their uncalled-for raucousness and head for the two empty chairs at the table.

As I pull out a chair for Chelsea, I ask, "Where are Derek and Diana?"

"They left yesterday," Avery says. "They have jobs and a teenager to wrangle. Besides, this isn't a party week. You guys need to get whipped into shape for the big match."

I sink onto my chair and groan. "No one warned me what this charity event was really about."

Chelsea elbows me in the side. "Don't be a grump."

"Who, me? I am never grumpy."

Hugh and Avery laugh with too much enthusiasm. When they finally stop doing that, Hugh rises from his chair. "We have an announcement to make this morning. Dominic and Chelsea are now officially a couple. Took them bloody long enough to stop living in denial."

Before I can snarl at him, his wife rises to stand beside him. "Everyone lift your glasses and drink a toast to the new couple."

I suddenly realize we all have glasses of champagne. This is overkill, but I won't complain and risk being labeled a grump again.

After breakfast, it's time for the training to begin in earnest. I ate light, so I'd be ready to go. The Sommerleigh estate has a spacious lawn that can accommodate our practice sessions, and a pitch has been set up in the middle of it. Last time I'd been here, during Hugh and Avery's wedding week festivities, we had played cricket—but without a real pitch. Now, we have an official one made of clay loam. I step onto the flat surface, surprised by its uniformity and how it has exactly the right amount of bounce.

My teammates arrive while I'm still standing in the middle of the pitch.

Benno Hochberg jogs up to me and slaps my arm. "Worried you can't keep up with the younger men?"

"No." Maybe I am, but I refuse to admit that to Benno.

Once all the players have arrived, Chip Martel whistles to get our attention. "Listen up, mates. It's time to welcome our democratically elected team captain."

Why wasn't I informed of the vote? Not that I would have argued about who should have the job. Any of these men could handle it.

Chip grins. "Three cheers for our captain, Dominic Rigby!"

Chapter Eighteen

Chelsea

I want to watch the first training session, but I'm afraid Dominic might get more anxious if he catches me observing. Avery and Rosalyn relax on lawn chaises that Kendall brought out for them, and they unabashedly watch the men brushing up on their skills. The guys discuss strategy too. I heard the announcement that Dom will be the team captain, though I'm sure he's not entirely pleased with that development. If he can coach schoolgirls, he can definitely handle this group of cocky former cricketers.

When I start to head for the house, Avery catches up to me. "Where are you going? I thought you'd want to watch the boys practicing."

"Don't think Dom would appreciate that. My presence might make him nervous."

"I doubt that. Even if it is true, he needs your support to see him through the big event." She turns toward the lawn. "Come on, Chelsea. You can sit with me and Rosalyn."

"Well…okay."

Avery shepherds me to the shady edge of the lawn, close to the house, but I only see two chaises. Before I can ask Avery about that, Kendall appears, carrying another chaise. Now I can sit with Avery and Rosalyn. Kendall fetches drinks for the three of us too—rhubarb cordials, a delicious nonalcoholic option. That man is more than a butler. He's a treasure. I hope the Parrishes pay him very well.

Dominic notices me, and he smiles tightly.

I wave and blow him a kiss.

He screws up one side of his mouth and waves. Then he turns away to talk to his teammates.

"Do you guys know much about cricket?" I ask Avery and Rosalyn. "I've watched matches, but I still think the sport is very confusing and bizarre."

"It is," Rosalyn says. "That's why we love it. Cricket is a quintessentially British sport."

"No matter how many matches I see, I still don't understand the game. The rules are…kind of insane."

"Yes, dear, they are. But I assumed Dominic would have explained the game to you."

"He tried." I glance out at the pitch, where the men are still gathered while engaged in discussion. "I know when to cheer for him, and that's about it."

Rosalyn pats my arm. "That's all you need to know, dear. My husband loved cricket, and I cheered for him at every match despite not having a bloody clue what was going on most of the time. My son has little interest in the game."

"But Hugh played cricket during the wedding week stuff."

"That's true," Avery says. "My husband likes to take part in an informal match on occasion. But he's not into the professional version of cricket."

"Dominic loved competing internationally. Sometimes I feel like a horrible friend because I don't love the game that means so much to him."

"Friend? You guys are more than that now."

We announced our new relationship status just this morning, so I guess I haven't gotten used to talking about us that way. "I meant back when we were just friends and I went to matches to watch him play."

I take a long drink of my rhubarb cordial as I try to figure out what the men are doing out there. Finally, they break up their huddle and scatter around the lawn, aka the cricket field, though

Dominic and Colton stay by the pitch. Dom scans the area as if he's looking for something—or someone.

He cups his hands like a megaphone and hollers, "Hugh! Where the bloody hell are you? We're ready to go."

A figure sprints past our chaises. Hugh carries an armful of things I can't identify as he hustles over to the pitch. Dominic and Colton take two of those items—protective pads, I now see. Those will shield them while they're batting. Hugh drops more protective pads on the ground so he can hand each man a bat. That's another weird thing about cricket. Superficially, it resembles baseball, but the bats are wide and flat instead of rounded.

Dominic and Colton strap on their protective gear.

Hugh does the same and also straps on an abdominal guard, then he excavates a red ball from his pants pocket. That would be the cricket ball. I have to admit I like those. They're pretty. I told Dom that once, and he called me "an American heathen who doesn't understand the sacred game." He was teasing me, of course.

Colton and Hugh approach one wicket. Dom takes the other.

"Shouldn't there be two umpires?" I ask. "I mean, there are two wickets."

"You are correct," Rosalyn tells me. "But the two teams agreed that one umpire would be chosen by each team and the two would serve throughout the match. Hugh is filling in until Dane Dixon can join us next week."

I know Dominic and Dane have been friends for a long time, so it doesn't surprise me at all that Dane will participate in the charity match. I've met him a few times, and he's an interesting guy—and a billionaire, like Diana.

"For the big event," Avery says, "they'll be playing a T20 match, which is the shortest version of cricket. Test cricket lasts for five days."

"Get your arse in position, wicketkeeper," Dominic shouts. "I'm talking to you, Banks. Quit staring at the ladies."

Will Banks jogs over to the pitch, taking up his position a little ways behind a wicket, crouching there. Hugh and Colton are waiting at the other wicket, but something is missing. I'm about to speak up when Dom issues another order.

"O'Hara, you can't bowl from the outfield. Honestly, you lot are worse than the little girls I coach. And what are you doing so close to the pitch, Roydon? You're a fielder."

Declan O'Hara rushes over to where Hugh and Colton stand while Glen Roydon sprints further away to take up his assigned spot. Lord Sommerleigh hovers behind Declan as the Irishman takes his position in front of the umpire. Glen Roydon jogs over to his assigned position.

I can't deny that watching and listening to Dominic ordering his teammates around makes me so hot for him. It doesn't take much to do that, though. Everything about him turns me on.

Dom raises his bat, knees bent, and waits for Declan to bowl. Americans like me know it as pitching, though the cricket version seems to have little in common with baseball. Not that I'm an expert on that either.

Ball in hand, Declan just stands there. I assume he's calculating the best trajectory for his bowl. Finally, he throws the ball.

Dom swings his bat—and misses. The ball smacks into the bails, the wooden crosspieces on the wicket, and knocks them down.

"He's out," Rosalyn informs me. "In a regular match, he would have to leave the field. But this is practice. I assume Dominic will try again, as many times as necessary until he finds his footing."

Poor Dominic. I want to race over there to hug him, but I doubt he would appreciate that. He needs to focus on his technique. One of the first things I ever learned about him was that he does not give up easily. That's why I can't understand his anxiety about the charity match. Now that he's on the field again, I bet he'll find his footing faster than even he expected.

Colton approaches Dom, and the two engage in a hushed conversation. Their intense expressions suggest they're talking about how to improve Dom's batting. In cricket, they call the batter a batsman, which I think is much sexier than the American term.

Dominic nods once.

Colton slaps his arm and heads back to the other wicket, where Declan waits to bowl again. The wicketkeeper, Will Banks, tosses the ball back to Declan. Then the Irishman bowls again.

With a fierce expression on his face, Dominic swings his bat—and misses again. This time, the ball sails over the wicket, and the wicketkeeper catches it. Dom sets the tip of his bat on the ground and bows his head.

Colton rushes over to talk to him again.

Dominic shakes his head, scowling, and drops his bat. He shoves his hands into his hair.

Hugh and Declan trot to the other end of the pitch, and Hugh claps a hand on Dom's shoulder while speaking to him. Dom nods but still seems upset.

Lord Sommerleigh hurries across the field to where I and the other two ladies have been relaxing on our chaises. He leans over, speaking in a hushed voice. "Dominic needs you. He might not know it yet, but he does."

"What can I do? I'm not a cricket expert."

"He needs *you*, not a strategy session."

I finally get what he means, I think. So I jump up and follow Hugh out onto the field. He retakes his position as umpire while I approach Dominic at the other end of the pitch. Declan loiters near Hugh, but Colton simply moves behind the wicket at this end to give Dominic and me a bit of privacy.

"What's wrong?" I ask, and I keep my voice soft enough that no one else will hear. "You've never missed a ball before."

"Not true. Before I met you, I missed the occasional ball. Then I started practicing like a demon until I knew there was no way I would never be out again."

And I never have seen him strike out before. But he hasn't played a serious game in years. Today, he's playing against other re-tired cricketers, but soon, he will be pitted against younger, better trained men. They probably practice every day year-round.

What can I do to ease Dom's anxiety? I can't drag him down onto the pitch and screw him, which doesn't leave me with many options. But maybe I don't need a drastic solution. Maybe all he needs is encouragement from someone who loves him.

I clasp his hands. "Listen to me, Dom. You are not a has-been. You're not even the oldest man on the team. Sure, you're older than the aver-age cricketer, but you've kept in shape, and you are ready for this."

"Can't even bat properly anymore."

"Bullshit. I've seen you coach girls who had never played the game before and whip them into shape in one morning. And I've watched you turn this ragtag group of ex-players into a team in a matter of minutes." I grasp his face with both hands. "You are amazing, in every way. Stop second-guessing yourself. Stop thinking, period. Listen to your instincts and your heart."

"My heart won't win a match."

"Yes, it will. You love this game, and that love is what made you The Dom."

He stares at me for a moment, then straightens and squares his shoulders. Lifting his chin, he curls his lips into a naughty smile that makes his eyes seem to glitter. "I am going to need to shag you later."

I rub my thumb over his bottom lip. "Hit every ball with no outs and your wish will come true."

"Are you saying you won't let me fuck you if I crash and burn?"

"Gotta give you some kind of incentive, right?" I peck a kiss on his lips and trot back to my chaise.

The players resume their positions, and Declan bowls.

Dominic swings his bat. The whack of the wood striking the ball echoes across the whole field and off the walls of the house. As the ball sails across the field, Dominic and Colton run across the pitch, switching places, then turn around and do it again before the ball touches down at the far side of the field.

Everyone cheers or whoops, and some jump up and down while doing that. Dom's teammates rush over to the pitch and swarm him.

I spring out of my chaise, screaming and clapping. My heart races, and I want to go over there to congratulate Dominic, but I don't want to interrupt his teammates efforts to show how much they love him. Men would never phrase it that way, but women know the truth. Dom's friends not only love him, they respect him too.

When the crowd finally disperses, I bolt for the pitch and fling my entire body at Dominic. He catches me, stumbling backward a step, and chuckles.

"I didn't win the World Cup," he says. "I managed to hit the ball after two outs. That's nothing to celebrate. The uproar is unwarranted."

"No way." I kiss him hard. "You got your mojo back. The Dom is ready to destroy those youngsters in a match that will be a blood bath."

He grins and laughs with even more vigor. "You're barmy, but I love that about you."

I slide down his body until my feet touch the ground. We look at each other, and I swear something zings between us. I can't describe it, and I don't need to, because I know exactly what this is.

I am in love with Dominic Rigby.

Chapter Nineteen

Dominic

My teammates retake their positions, but I just stand here basking in the glory of hitting the fucking ball at last, for the first time in years. I hadn't tried until now, not really. The match we played at Sommerleigh a few months ago didn't involve official rules. We did it for fun. But when that ball cracked on my bat, I experienced an adrenaline rush like nothing I'd ever felt before, not even during a World Cup match.

Though my team hadn't won the World Cup, we pulled off incredible feats of cricketing. I don't care if that's hyperbole. I've bloody well earned the right to be overdramatic. But I know this team has a lot of work to do yet if we mean to trounce the younger blokes.

"Back to your positions," I shout. "Practice doesn't end because I hit the ball."

My mates hurry back to their positions.

Since this is practice, we aren't counting overs or kicking anyone off the field for getting out. That's why I'm still here after two misses. But we can't waste time. After a few days of unregulated practice, we will need to refresh our knowledge of the rules and then stick to them.

I've never coached adults before. That thought trickles unease through me. But then I glance at Chelsea, and she smiles, and all of those worries disintegrate. I stand up straighter. She gives me the thumbs-up sign, which spurs me to lift my chin and thump my bat on my palm.

After a long day of practice, with only a quick meal of sandwiches and potato crisps for lunch, I tell my teammates to finish with their favorite cool-down routine and then do whatever they want. I don't even admonish them against drinking alcohol. As long as they don't get pissed, I won't stop them.

I go to my room and take a shower, fantasizing that Chelsea might join me, but she doesn't. She has a job to do too.

When I amble into the dining room, I halt just past the doorway. "Where is everyone? Did my team leg it already?"

Hugh sits at the head of the table with Avery at his left and Rosalyn at his right. Chelsea occupies the chair opposite those three. No one else is here.

"They're in their rooms," Hugh says. "You wore out those men, but that's exactly what you needed to do. Isn't it? I'm hardly an expert on coaching."

"Neither am I, except with young girls. They're easier to control then grown men, unless they develop a crush on me."

"Which they all do," Chelsea says. She pats the chair beside her. "Come sit down."

I settle onto the seat. "Not every student feels that way about me."

"You really are determined to ignore the signs. But I've seen how those girls look at you, whether they're twelve or seventeen or somewhere in the middle. You are their rock star."

"Bollocks. I can't sing or play an instrument."

Chelsea gives me a patient smile. "You've been teaching at a girls' school for years. You must have noticed the way they all gaze at you dreamily."

"Perhaps Dom isn't ready to accept the truth yet," Hugh says. "Let's eat and talk about something else."

I throw my head back and groan. "Yes, please, any other subject will do."

"Wonderful. Tell us about your plans for training your team this week."

Maybe we should go back to discussing schoolgirls and their supposed crushes on me.

Fortunately, Avery changes the subject—deftly. I've never seen anyone manage other people as well as she does, but I imagine an image consultant needs to develop that sort of skill. When I mention that I wish I had her talent for dealing with people, Avery raises her brows.

"You already have that skill," she says. "I watched you handling your team today, and I was very impressed. You're a natural leader, Dominic."

Natural? Me?

I shake my head at Hugh. "Did you let your wife drink an entire bottle of vodka before dinner? She must be drunk to make a claim like that."

"Lady Sommerleigh never gets drunk." He squints his eyes and flattens his lips. "I might need to punch you for suggesting such a thing."

The way his lips ticked upward at the corners lets me know he won't actually do that. Avery knows I was joking, I'm sure, and so does Hugh. Our group of mates have developed a strange dynamic in which we threaten to assault or murder each other as a type of humor. The Scots I've met do the same thing. That's probably why Hugh and Callum MacTaggart became friends.

After dinner, Chelsea and I trudge up the stairs. We're both completely knackered, so we say goodnight and retreat to our separate rooms. We had left the adjoining door open, though, and that means we can sneak into each other's rooms in the middle of the night if one of us develops a sudden, powerful urge to shag.

That doesn't happen, however. Neither of us wakes up until morning, and then we're called to breakfast by Kendall. He politely raps on my door, then Chelsea's, as if he doesn't know we have adjoining rooms. I'm positive the butler does know, but he's too polite to admit that.

Chelsea eats heartily, but I need to keep my meal light. A full English would ruin my game today. But once we play the charity match, I plan to devour a three-course meal with desserts. Not that I have a clue what a meal like that involves. But it sounds like would include a lot of food.

After breakfast, I kiss Chelsea goodbye and march out to our makeshift cricket ground. Sommerleigh doesn't have an actual stadium, of course, but my mind conjures up memories of the locations I'd played in over the years, from India to Australia and America too. The United States doesn't really do cricket grounds, not to the extent and grandeur of English ones.

I remember every match, especially the ones I played at Lord's. That stadium will always be my favorite because my very first professional match took place there. But I doubt I'll ever play at Lord's again. I'm not in the game anymore. This charity match will be my final appearance in the world of cricket.

Maybe I am a bit sad about that. But only a little.

Just like yesterday, I arrive before the other blokes. I test the pitch, but it feels exactly right. Then I walk the entire infield and outfield to make sure the grass is still perfectly mowed. I don't need to do this. I enjoy it, that's all. As a coach, I've made it part of my daily routine to check every last inch of the playing surface before any match.

The smell of the grass invigorates me. It always has done.

But Chelsea invigorates me more than anything else on earth. Knowing she believes in me…that's the only reason I haven't bowed out of the charity match. I wish it hadn't taken me years to realize how much I love her.

My teammates emerge from the house just as I've returned to the pitch. "Ready to go, gents? We need to train hard today, so we can take a holiday tomorrow."

"Does that mean we get to go back to London tomorrow?" Mickey Randall asks. "My wife misses me already."

"You can do whatever you like on your day off, but please behave yourselves. I don't want to hear about you lot staying up till all hours and getting pissed."

"So that's what Brits do?" Benno Hochberg asks. "I thought you people were uptight and virtuous. Germans know how to enjoy life without giving ourselves hangovers."

I flash him a sarcastic look of disapproval. "I believe you're confusing Brits with Germans. You people worship beer, after all. You even hold festivals devoted to it."

Will Banks raises his hand.

"You don't need permission," I say. "Go on and speak."

"Are we going to train today? Or make a lot of jokes?"

"Of course we're going to train." I wave for them all to approach the pitch. "I want each and every one of you to get back up to speed with every position. I'm sure we're all a bit rusty. That way, if someone should get injured, we'll have qualified substitutes. That means you'll need to work very hard. Any complaints about that?"

Eleven heads shake.

"Good." I pick up the bat I'd left on the pitch. "Let's start with batsman. That is the most important position to play. I'm going have you practice batting in pairs. That way you can get used to making runs and switching out even if you've never been a batsman before. Any questions?"

Those eleven heads shake again.

"Brilliant." I set my foot on the ball I'd left on the pitch. "Martel, you will bowl. Roydon and Carter, you are the batsman, and Roydon will bat first. Pull on your protective gear, and we'll get started."

Carter and Roydon grab the protective gear I'd left on the grass for them, while Martel takes a pair of those and an abdominal guard.

I pass the bat to Roydon. "Show us what you can do. If I'm not thoroughly impressed, you won't bat in the charity match."

"Whatever you say, skipper."

Martel takes two big breaths, then pulls his arm back and surges forward to release the ball and send it sailing across the pitch. Roydon swings and hits the ball, but it slams straight into the wicket at the other end.

I casually walk up to the batsman. "Tell me, Roydon, did that look like a good hit?"

"Well, it wasn't the worst ever. Was it?" He winces. "It was total rubbish."

"Yes. Try again. I'll give you three more chances to improve."

"Thanks, skipper." Roydon grins and hurries over to the broken wicket, where he helps set it right. Then he returns to his end of the pitch. "Try number two, eh?"

"Whenever the bowler is ready."

Martel hurls another ball, and this time, Roydon doesn't knock the bails off when he swings. Instead, he loses control of his bat, and it flies onto the infield.

I resist the urge to cover my face with my hands. "Two more tries."

After failing twice more, Roydon hands the bat back to me. "Sorry, skipper. I'm not cut out for being a batsman, am I?"

"No. But I watched you yesterday, and I think you'll excel as a fielder."

"Really? That's brilliant."

Grinning, he leaves the pitch to join his mates.

I spend the entire morning figuring out who belongs in each position and who might serve as a substitute in case a player suffers an injury or has to leave the field due to an out.

Blimey. This is more grueling than I expected.

At last, I'm able to announce good news. "It's time for lunch!"

The team erupts in shouts of joy and takes off running for the house.

"Don't eat too much," I shout. "Can't practice when you're vomiting all over the field."

I join everyone a few minutes later for a light lunch. Chelsea is there, of course, and she sits right next to me. Several times, she sneaks a hand under the table to squeeze my thigh, and I struggle to pretend I'm not getting aroused by what she's doing. Luckily, no one else notices. We leave the dining room together, before the others have gone, and Chelsea takes hold of my hand to guide me into the solarium.

"What are we doing here?" I ask.

"Making plans."

"For what?"

She raises onto her tiptoes and leans into me. "Our first outdoor shag."

I can't come up with a response, at least not one that wouldn't sound like gibberish.

"Why are you surprised?" she asks. "Having sex on the cricket pitch was your idea."

"Yes, but I didn't think you would actually agree to that."

"I do agree. And I want us to get naked on the pitch tonight."

Chapter Twenty

Chelsea

Come on, Dominic. We both know you want this as much as I do, so say yes." I roll my hips forward to rub myself into his groin, earning a sharp grunt from him. "Thinking about what we're planning to do tonight will keep you going during the long afternoon of training your team."

"Yes, it will do that for sure." He shuts his eyes briefly when I roll my hips again. "Bloody hell. I want you tonight, but I can't promise I'll stay awake after dinner. Training is more grueling than I remember. Of course, I was never the captain or the coach back then."

"Take a nap before dinner. Then you'll be awake and raring to go once everyone else has gone to bed."

"You've thought this through, haven't you? It isn't a spur of the moment suggestion."

"Nope. I've been thinking about this all morning."

He tips his head to the side, studying me. "I expected you and the other ladies to observe our training again today. But that would be rather boring the second time, I gather."

"We aren't bored with watching sexy men get sweaty and dirty. But I needed some help to prepare for the next photo shoot for the calendar. Avery and Rosalyn were more than happy to help."

Dominic blows out a breath. "More photos."

"That's right. More photos to collect money for cancer research." I kiss him, letting our lips linger against each other for a long moment. "You'll be rewarded in the most satisfying ways I can think of."

"Well, that does make it worthwhile. When will you need me again? For more pictures, that is."

"Tomorrow." I wrap my arms around his neck. "But I need you tonight for something else."

He smirks. "I won't miss that."

"Sex on the pitch tonight." I back away from him. "See you at dinner."

Avery and I meet up on the patio to discuss preparations for the big event. I'm not an expert on organizing massive gatherings or gala balls, but Avery insisted I should be in on the arrangements. My role as photographer for the calendar does not, as she informs me, mean that I can't take on other roles. She wants me to be the photographer for the gala too. On top of that, she asks me to become her right hand in pretty much everything about the charity extravaganza.

But while we're discussing the logistics of the charity events, I ask what seems like an innocuous question. "Where will the match take place? No one has mentioned that. I don't think even Dominic knows."

"Yeah, we kept that on the down low. Hugh was worried that Dominic might freak out when he learns which venue we booked."

A slight chill slithers through my veins. "Which venue?"

"Lord's."

I stare at her without blinking, and every hair on my arms and my nape stiffens. "Lord's Cricket Ground? That's a massive stadium. How many people are you expecting to show up?"

"We've sold out the stadium. That means over thirty thousand spectators."

Dom has been anxious about playing again after years of retirement. How will he react when he finds out he'll be playing in a giant venue? The most famous one in England? I know he competed in matches at Lord's during his professional career, and I even attended one of them. It's the premier cricket ground in England, maybe even the world. What if Dom panics at the prospect of returning to that stadium?

"Let me break the news to Dominic," I say. "He's been worried about competing against younger, better trained men. Now we're talking about Dom and his team playing inside a famous stadium."

"Of course. You should break it to him."

"I know Dom can handle it, but he might not be so sure."

Avery smiles. "Men often need women to help them see the light."

Once we finish making plans for the big events, I go outside to see how the cricketers are doing. I need to talk to Dominic, but I don't want to interrupt their training. So I linger near the corner of the house to watch. After about ten minutes, they conclude their training session, and everyone except Dominic goes inside the house. He stays behind and stands there with his hands on his hips and his head bowed, seeming to be studying the grass.

I come up beside him. "Are all the blades in the right position?"

He jerks his head up. "What blades?"

"The grass. It seemed like you were staring at it, so I figured you must be counting the blades."

"No, I wasn't doing that. I've been thinking about strategies for getting my team ready for the big match."

"I have some news on that front."

He raises his brows.

"Don't freak out, okay?" I move closer to rest a hand on his arm. "I know you've been anxious about competing against younger men who have been training for years. But this could be a good thing."

"What could be? The fact that I'm ancient, in sports terms?"

"No." I take a deep breath and tell him. "The charity match will take place at Lord's."

Dominic's face goes blank. He doesn't blink, and I'm starting to think he might not be breathing either. Just when I decide I need to smack Dom to wake him up, he blinks several times quickly, rousing himself from his frozen state. "Lord's?"

"Yes."

He shakes his head slowly. Then his lips curl up a touch at the corners. He slings an arm around me, pulling me snugly against his side. And he grins. "That's wonderful! The very first professional match I ever played took place at Lord's. I was thinking about that earlier today." His grin widens, and he starts to laugh. "This is incredible news."

"You aren't going to panic? Lord's Cricket Ground holds more than thirty thousand spectators."

"I might have been worried if you'd told me the news a few days ago. But today I realized that even if we lose the match, we will still win. It's all for charity, anyway." He gives me a little squeeze and plants a quick, hard kiss on my mouth. "What you did for me yesterday helped more than you could possibly imagine. And my team has worked bloody hard to get in match condition. Whatever the outcome, we will know we did our best."

"Glad to hear that. But what did I do yesterday?"

"You convinced me I could do this. No one else could have talked me down from my disgust with myself after I cocked up my swings. I was on the verge of deciding someone else needs to be batsman. Thank you, Chelsea."

"All I did was give you a pep talk."

"Oh no, you did much more than that." He kisses me again. "You inspired me."

"I'm happy to do that again whenever you need it." I lay a hand on his chest. "So, are we still on for our private game tonight?"

"Absolutely." He takes my hand, leading me toward the house. "This might sound barmy, but playing at Lord's again feels like destiny."

"I don't think that's crazy at all. You're going back to where your career began, and I have an intuition that you retirees will beat the pants off the younger guys."

He raises our joined hands to kiss my knuckles. "I know better than to second guess any woman, but especially you, darling."

We join the rest of the gang in the dining room for a lavish dinner. Since the cricketers have tomorrow off, the Parrishes decided they deserved a feast this evening as a reward for their hard work. I devour all the delicious foods on offer, but I stop short of overdoing it. Don't want to get bloated when I have a sex date with Dominic later. We both eat dessert, and the decadent treat has the odd effect of making me horny. I suppose that's because of Dominic, not really because of the food. He keeps whispering things in my ear that aren't dirty but that make me shiver with excitement simply because he spoke in a rough, sensual tone.

After dinner, we go to our adjoining rooms and watch TV on my bed while we wait for everyone else to go to sleep. It takes longer than I'd anticipated. The cricketers seem to have decided a day off tomorrow means partying tonight. Lord Sommerleigh knocks on the door three hours after the cricketers got their party started. I still hear the raucous laughter as I open the door.

"Hi, Hugh. What's up?"

"Those ruddy cricketers, that's what. I'm sorry they're making so much noise. Mum can sleep through fireworks going off right outside the house, but my wife has had enough. I assume you have too."

"They are boisterous, for sure."

"I was hoping Dominic might help me tame the wild cricketers. He is in here, isn't he?"

"Yes." I glance over my shoulder. "Dom, Hugh needs your help."

"They are your team, after all," Hugh calls out. "Get your arse out here so we can subdue those rowdy blokes. Can't do it alone."

"I could help," I suggest.

Dom comes up behind me. "No, you cannot, Chelsea. Controlling eleven rowdy men who have probably raided the drinks cabinet is not a job for a beautiful woman. That lot would harass you with endless attempts to flirt with and seduce you."

"Oh, please. I know how to deal with drunken men."

"Stay here, pet. I'll take care of this."

I try very hard not to laugh at that statement because I can tell he means it. Dominic seriously worries about what his teammates might do if I go down there. I think our new relationship status has made him overprotective. "Okay, I will let you men handle the situation."

Dom kisses my cheek and leaves with Hugh. I probably should shut the door and stare at the TV, but I'm curious about what will happen downstairs. I promised to "stay here," but that's awfully vague. The wording of my vow gives me plenty of wiggle room, and I'm dying to listen in on Dominic and Hugh's attempt to corral the cricketers. So I interpret Dom's statement to mean that I can hover on the landing at the top of the stairs to eavesdrop. What? I'm still "here," as in upstairs and in close proximity to our adjoining rooms.

The lights in the downstairs hall are on, so I can see Dominic and Hugh as they approach the closed door to the dining room.

Hugh pushes one half of the double doors open. "Beddy-bye time, gents. Set down the liquor bottles and go to your rooms."

Movement to my left draws my attention, and I catch Avery tiptoeing over here. She stops right beside me and holds up a pair of binoculars. "Wanna spy?"

"Absolutely."

She hands me the binoculars. "You can go first."

"Thanks."

I raise the binoculars and adjust the focus until I can see the interior of the dining room clearly, though I only have a view of part of the room. Damn, I wish Hugh had opened both sides of the door. Dominic has just followed Hugh into the dining room. I've lost sight of Lord Sommerleigh, but I have a good view of Dom. He shakes his head, his lips warping into a half frown, half smile.

"You lot are incorrigible," he says. "What did you do? Raid the refrigerator and the drinks cabinet?"

"The pantry too, I'm sure." That's Hugh talking.

Fortunately, the acoustics in this house ensure that Avery and I can hear what Dominic and Hugh are saying, though the responses from the cricketers are difficult to make out.

"Maybe we should sneak partway down the stairs," I whisper. "Then we could hear better."

"Yes, we should eavesdrop."

That is not Avery's voice. We both glance back at Rosalyn.

"You want to spy?" I ask. "A proper British lady like you?"

"Of course I do." She snatches the binoculars from me. "This is the best entertainment I've had in years. Perhaps one of those cricketers will remove his shirt. Benno looks like he would have spectacular abs."

A woman of the peerage wants to ogle young men's bodies? My mouth must be gaping because I can't believe she suggested such a thing.

Avery whispers into my ear, "Rosalyn loves men. She shamelessly admired Derek's body when she first met him."

Rosalyn edges past us, heading down the stairs. "Forget the binoculars, ladies. We need close-up views of what's going on down there."

Chapter Twenty-One

Dominic

Glen Roydon climbs onto the dining room table and begins to dance, pumping his hips and shouting "woo-yeah" while he attempts to turn in a circle. But he doesn't have the equilibrium for that. The moron can barely stand upright, which means he's at risk of tumbling to the floor and potentially injuring himself. We need all team members on the field for the big match at Lord's.

Hugh is busy trying to collect all the liquor bottles, presumably so he can take them away and lock them up in the drinks cabinet, wherever that is.

Sighing, I approach the table and grasp Glen's ankle. "Stop, Roydon. It's time to go to bed before you vomit all over the antique dining table."

No idea if it's actually an antique. But I'm hoping he will stop this nonsense if he thinks it might cost him a fortune. He wouldn't want to pay to replace the broken table.

"You're a stick in the muck, Rigby," Glen says, his words a bit slurred. "Didn't Shelly shag you yet?"

"Her name is Chelsea, and you are behaving like a ruddy arsehole. The phrase is 'stick in the *mud*,' by the way."

"Bugger off, would you? I'm having fun."

I glance at Hugh, but he can't seem to push past the inebriated cricketers to remove the alcohol from the room. I ought to help him, but first I need to deal with Glen. "I'll give you a full bottle of booze if you get off the table, Roydon."

No, I won't actually do that. I'm lying, but that seems acceptable in this situation.

Benno Hochberg is lying flat on his back on the floor, snoring like a rusty chainsaw. In the far corner, Terry Cash and Mickey Randall seem to be playing pat-a-cake while giggling like schoolgirls. A few others wander about aimlessly, and several keep sloppily hounding Hugh in an attempt to steal the liquor bottles from him. Chip Martel slouches in the chair at the head of the table, where Lord Sommerleigh always sits at dinner.

I finally manage to drag Glen Roydon off the table and leave him slumped in a chair. Then I approach Chip. "What are you doing? I left you in charge of the 'after party,' as you called it. You swore to me you wouldn't drink."

He lifts his gaze to me, blinking slowly, his eyes glassy and his face flushed. "I tried not to. But Wortham dared me to drink vodka with Tabasco sauce in it."

Oh yes, his speech is slurred too.

"Someone dared you, so naturally, you got completely pissed. It makes perfect sense." I smack the back of his head. "I trusted you. And you behaved like a fucking schoolboy. Stay where you are. I'll deal with you later, Martel."

I head over to where Hugh is still struggling to maintain control of the liquor bottles. Suddenly, the men surrounding him freeze and swerve their attention to the doorway. As if they're all psychically connected, they simultaneously break into sloppy grins and stagger toward the doorway.

Hugh compresses his lips and narrows his gaze. "Don't you bastards touch my wife."

I whirl around and see three women hovering just outside the doorway. Chelsea, Avery, and Rosalyn go wide-eyed as the drunkards blunder closer to them. I rush over there and blockade the doorway with my body, facing the completely pissed horde. "Stop right there or I'll punch each and every one of you so hard you'll be useless lumps on the floor."

The staggering horde shuffles to a halt.

"Very good. Now stay right where you are."

I raise onto my toes to peer over the cricketers' heads, searching for Hugh. He can't get past the crowd, though he has set down the liquor bottles. I glance over my shoulder. "Ladies, please return to your rooms. Hugh and I will deal with the plastered arses."

"We can help," Chelsea says. "Do you have any idea how many drunk boys I dealt with in college?"

"Please go back to your rooms, ladies. These idiots are my responsibility."

"Of course, you are correct," Rosalyn says. "We will return to our quarters and let you two handle these men. Won't we, girls?"

"Sure," Chelsea says, and Avery echoes her statement.

The women retreat upstairs.

And I slam the dining room door shut.

Every man except Hugh stumbles backward.

Lord Sommerleigh chuckles. "Oh yes, you lot are in serious trouble. The Dom is displeased with his teammates."

I glower at the men. "You can forget about having a day off. Better ring your wives or girlfriends to tell them why you can't visit them tomorrow. Leave is canceled."

Chip Martel tries to push up straighter in his chair but sinks down again. "I, uh, don't have a girlfriend or wife. Does that mean I can still go on leave?"

"No, you bloody moron. All of you are staying here." I jab a finger at him. "And you are guilty of dereliction of duty."

He sinks deeper into his chair. "Sorry, skipper. Won't happen again."

"Better adhere to that vow," Hugh says. "Dominic doesn't seem like the sort who forgives a second time."

"That's right," I say. "If you ever want to drink more than water or apple juice, do not annoy me this way ever again."

What have I learned from teaching at a girls' school? One must always make a punishment sound severe, otherwise no one will stop their bad behavior.

"All right," I say with a sigh. "Time for bed. And I will be locking you in your rooms tonight."

Hugh lifts his brows at me.

I shrug. Then I fling the door open and step aside. "Off with the lot of you. Now."

My fellow cricketers shamble across the hall and up the stairs. I hear door after door slam shut until the house finally falls into silence. Once everyone is tucked in for the night, figuratively speaking, I face Hugh. "We should put away the liquor."

"No need, sir." Kendall appears on the other side of the doorway, making me jump and nearly giving me a heart attack. "I heard the commotion but thought I should wait until it died down before I cleaned up after that lot."

"Those morons are my charges. I will clean up after them."

"Please, sir, it's my job. You must be knackered after a hard day of training."

Hugh approaches us. "Yes, Dom, let Kendall do his job. He knows precisely where everything in this house belongs, whereas you and I would probably stash the bottles in the wrong cabinet."

"All right, we'll leave it to you, Kendall."

The butler nods crisply. "Thank you, sir."

As Hugh and I mount the stairs, he asks me, "Are you really going to lock them in their rooms?"

"No, of course not. They're all so drunk they'll pass out the second their heads meet their pillows. In the morning, they'll be feeling very contrite."

"Do you employ that tactic with your students?"

"A slightly different version of it." I smirk. "Threatening to confiscate their mobiles does the trick."

Hugh turns down the hallway to head for the Lord and Lady's bedroom. I stop and wait until he disappears, then I sneak into Chelsea's room. Well, it's sort of become our bedroom.

Chelsea lies on the bed, on her side with all her clothes and even her shoes on, and her head propped up with one arm. "I peeked out when those guys thundered down the hall in all directions—up to the top floor and out into the rooms on this floor. You really scared the shit out of them, didn't you?"

I perch on the bed's edge near her hip. "It doesn't take much effort to send drunk men running for cover."

"But you're damn sexy when you let The Dom come out to play. I want to rip your clothes off right now."

"Not until midnight, and not until we're on the pitch. There's a full moon tonight, and I'm looking forward to seeing you naked under the glow of the moon."

She nudges my arse with her foot. "I know you said you're happy the big match will happen at Lord's…"

"But you're worried I'll be anxious again as we get closer to the day."

"Can you read my mind?"

"Hardly. But we have known each other for a long time. I understand your mind, and you understand mine."

She leans over to check the clock on the nightstand. "An hour to go."

"What should we do in the meantime?"

"Don't you think everyone is all tucked in by now?"

I love the way she thinks—about everything. "Can't wait to get your hands on me, eh? Let's go outside and see if all the lights are off except for ours."

We sneak out of our room, pausing at the top of the staircase to make sure no one heard us. Then we hurry downstairs and out the back door, reaching the pitch in a matter of minutes. The moon casts its milky glow on everything, including Sommerleigh House and the large lawn that currently serves as a training ground for cricketers. I can't see any lights on in the house, except for the one in our adjoining rooms.

Perfect. We don't need to wait until midnight.

I pull Chelsea close. "Strip for me, love. Right now."

"You should go first."

"Uh-uh-uh. I've already stripped for you once, and it's only fair that you go first this time." I give her arse a gentle push. "Move onto the pitch and show me your best striptease."

She backs away, unbuttoning her blouse as she moves. Once she reaches the center of the pitch, she removes her blouse and tosses it toward me. I don't bother to catch it. I watch with rapt attention as she unbuttons her trousers and drags the zipper down inch by inch, teasing me with the possibility of what's to come. Yes, all right, I've seen her naked before. But this time is different. We've admitted our feelings for each other, so now we aren't simply doing each other a favor. We are reveling in a deeper bond.

Chelsea slips out of her shoes and shimmies out of her trousers, tossing them at me with her foot. She gets rid of her socks next. Now wearing only her bra and knickers, she rotates to give me her backside. Then she slowly unhooks every tiny clasp on that bra one by one while she gazes at me over her shoulder and bites her lip.

I suddenly realize I'm stroking my cock through my trousers.

She removes her bra and tosses it to me. Finally, she pushes her knickers down, letting them fall to her ankles, and kicks them away.

Her naked backside is beautiful, but I need more. "Turn around, pet. Show me all of you."

She spins around.

I scratch my chin, though I have no idea why, as I drink in the sight of her nude body. "Fuck, you're perfect."

"Your turn, Dom."

"All right." I saunter up to the pitch but draw out a distance between us, to make sure she sees everything. I reach for the button on my jeans, but I stop with it caught between my fingers. "Why don't you undress me?"

"I'd love to."

She sashays up to me, swaying those hips in a deliberate attempt to drive me insane, and shoos my fingers away from that button. But she doesn't unhook it. Instead, she tugs my shirt out of my waistband and takes it off over my head, flinging it away. "Get rid of your shoes, please."

I slip out of them—and my socks too.

Chelsea kneels before me. Her face hovers in front of my cock, which lies trapped in my jeans and boxer shorts, stiff as iron and ready to fuck her.

"What are you doing, love?" I ask. "You're meant to undress me."

"Mm-hm."

She lunges her head forward to seize my zipper between her teeth. I follow her movements as she tugs the zipper down, down, down, using only her teeth to do it. Once she's finished that task, she grasps the waistband of my jeans with the fingers of both hands, gradually dragging the denim down my thighs, over my knees, and down to my ankles.

I step out of the jeans. But I'm still wearing my boxer shorts.

She drags those down too.

As I get rid of the boxers, my cock throbs with the need to take her body. Chelsea opens her mouth and slants toward me, toward my erection that waves in front of her face. When she seems about to take me into her mouth, I scuffle backward a few steps.

"Not yet," I say. "You come first."

She licks her lips. "Mm, but I want to taste you so badly."

"Another time. Go to the wicket and rest your sexy arse against it."

"Which wicket?"

"Either one. Just do it quickly."

She trots to the wicket and sets her arse on it.

I stride up to her and drop to my knees. "Spread your legs for me."

She does that—and my mouth descends on her slick, hot flesh.

Chapter Twenty-Two

Chelsea

Dominic shoves his head between my thighs, lapping at my swollen flesh while grunting as if nothing on earth tastes as good as I do. The roughness of his hands on my thighs feels good, but the velvety swipes of his tongue and the way his evening stubble rasps against my skin feels even better. The sensations drive me wild. I'd been turned on big time the moment we reached the pitch, but now my entire body tingles and throbs in all the places where I need it to do that. His hair tickles my mound, making me gasp.

The wicket creaks softly.

I shove my hands into Dominic's hair, cradling him to my body. My breathing grows faster and heavier, and my fingernails must be scratching his scalp, but he either doesn't notice or doesn't care. My sex throbs. My nipples feel so sensitized that even the cool midnight breeze makes them ache. While Dom devours me, I gasp and cling to him, not giving a damn if the wicket shatters. He grows more enthusiastic, until the stumps of the wicket begin to shake. I cry out, clinging to Dom's head even as my heels keep lifting off the surface of the pitch.

The bails tumble down.

My body goes rigid. I have no control over my muscles anymore, and the orgasm about to explode inside me dictates everything I do. Well, that and Dominic. He licks faster and faster, then shifts his head so he's suckling my clit like he might die without the nourishment of my cream. His stubble rasps along my cleft, ratcheting up my excitement until I swear I'll pass out if the climax doesn't hit right now.

He thrusts two fingers inside me.

And I go off. I can't even scream, so overwhelmed by the pleasure that tiny gasps are all I can release. The pleasure ricochets up and down my nerves while I grip the wicket stumps hard enough to make my knuckles ache. Dom shoves both hands under me and lowers my body onto the pitch. He keeps pumping those fingers into me, though I can't see what he's doing. My eyes are squeezed shut so tightly that stars burst behind my lids. I hear the distinctive sound of foil ripping, then his cock fills me up. And my body takes command again, forcing me to tighten my inner muscles around him.

"Bloody hell," he snarls. "I can't—ah—fuck."

I peel my lids open just enough to see the desperate look on his face. He sets his hands on the clay loam at either side of me and punches into my body like the piston of a steam engine, pounding so hard and fast that my whole body bounces. Another orgasm strikes, and I wrap my arms and legs around him to ride out the most intense pleasure I've ever experienced.

Dominic growls as he thrusts into me one last time, holding still while he comes. Then he drops onto the pitch beside me. "I never knew cricket sex could be like this."

"Have you done it with other women?"

"No, only you. I fantasized about it once in a while, but the woman in my dreams was always you."

"But you still thought we were just friends."

He rolls onto his side and tweaks my nipple, earning a gasp from me. "You didn't realize the truth either. So tell me, did you ever have a sex dream that involved me?"

"Oh, yes, I did. Those were the hottest dreams ever."

"It seems like neither of us was willing to admit how much we wanted to fuck each other senseless."

A laugh bubbles out of me. "Yeah, I definitely wanted that. But it's easy to dismiss those fantasies when you've been friends with someone for so long. We're both blind idiots, aren't we?"

"That is in the past. Now we're idiots who have our eyes wide open." He smirks. "And your legs wide open."

I sit up and realize some of the clay is stuck to my skin, mostly on my backside. "Think I need a shower. Cricket sex was incredible, but clay in my hair and stuck to my ass is not cool."

"We both need to clean ourselves up."

I grin. "My room has a big shower."

He picks me up and races into the house, though he slows down when we reach the stairs. "Better sneak up there."

"Definitely."

Only after we've taken a long, hot shower together do we realize we left our clothes out on the lawn. Dom volunteers to retrieve them. I slide under the covers on the big bed to wait for him. He returns with our clothes only a few minutes later, breathing hard as if he ran the entire way, except for the stairs. I would've heard his thumping footfalls if he ran up the steps.

He tosses our stuff on the floor and crawls into bed with me.

Dom lies on his back, so I sprawl half on top of him. I fall asleep faster than I would've expected, but I guess cricket sex really takes it out of a girl. The sunshine streaming through the windows inspires me to slowly wake up, stretch, and yawn, all while still sprawled over Dominic. After last night, I never want to wake up any other way.

A large hand covers half of my bottom.

I raise my head to look at Dominic, but he still has his eyes closed. His fingers, however, are exploring my ass. "You're not fooling me, mister. I know you're awake."

"Maybe my hands have become autonomous. It's not my fault if they want to feel you up."

"Better rise and shine, skipper. Your team needs you to whip them into shape."

He grunts and grudgingly opens his eyes. "They were so drunk last night that they'll surely be useless for cricket practice."

"So, you won't be giving them hell?"

"Oh, they'll get a piece of my mind. And I will force them to do some basic exercises, but not cricket related ones."

"Punishment exercises, hey?"

His lips twitch like he's trying not to smirk. "I can neither confirm nor deny that statement."

"Mind if I watch while you punish them?"

"That would be even better torture. Hungover arses jogging around the field while a beautiful woman observes."

We get dressed, eat breakfast with Hugh, Avery, and Rosalyn, and still don't see any sign of the cricketers who misbehaved last night. They must be very hungover. Dom heads upstairs to check on them, which means he pounds on their doors and yells for them to get their "arses" in gear. I'm still downstairs, but I swear I can hear a chorus of miserable groans echoing through the house. Even when Dom goes to the third floor to rouse the last of the men, I can hear his booming voice.

"Take showers before you leave your rooms," he hollers. "I want clean, wide awake faces the next time I see you."

Dominic jogs down the stairs. "What do you have planned today?"

"That depends on your plans. Will you work the cricketers until sundown?"

"No. I'll give them a brief workout, then let them relax for the rest of the day."

"Being a teacher makes you a better team captain, hey?"

"I suppose it does."

While he goes off to find Kendall and ask the butler to cook a light breakfast for the hungover athletes, I retrieve my equipment from the bedroom. I haven't shared my plans for today with Dominic. I didn't intentionally change the subject, but I doubt he'll be thrilled with my plans for the day.

By the time Dominic returns from the kitchen, I'm just coming down the staircase. He waits at the bottom with his hands in his jeans pockets and one hip cocked, looking casually hot. I stop on the last step. His big body blocks my way.

"What are your plans for the day?" he asks. "You never told me, and that makes me suspicious."

"Getting paranoid, huh? I want more photos of you."

He groans miserably. "More posing?"

"That's right. Your teammates need to recuperate, so today is the perfect time to get more shots of you."

He glances up the stairs. "I'd better check on those morons."

Dominic jogs up the staircase, disappearing from view.

My curiosity gets the better of me, and I linger at the bottom of the stairs to watch the cricketers skulk out of their rooms. It takes a few minutes before anyone emerges. Then they begin to appear, one by one, yawning and stretching, shuffling their feet. I've learned all their names and can recognize their faces too, so I list each one in my mind as they come downstairs.

Chip Martel. Benno Hochberg. Colton Ward. Gilbert Paquet. Mickey Randall. Declan O'Hara. Glen Roydon. Will Banks. Brian Wortham. Terry Cash. Hugo Carter.

Despite their pitiful state, every man summons a wan smile and greets me. Only after all the others have gone into the dining room does Dominic come back.

"When do you want me?" he asks. "For the photo session, I meant."

"No cricket sex today?"

"In the daytime? No. After dark...who knows." He pulls me close and kisses me. "Once the team has eaten breakfast, I'll give them their quick workout. Then I'm all yours."

"Great. Meet me in the garden when you're ready. And wear your cricket kit, please."

He bows deeply. "Whatever my lady wishes."

Wow, no bitching about posing for me this time. He even seems, dare I say, almost enthusiastic about it.

I hang out in the solarium with Rosalyn until I hear the cricketers leaving the house. I know it's them because Dominic's authoritative voice echoes in the hall as he encourages the other men to follow him. Since he told me the workout wouldn't last long, I carry my equipment out to the garden and set things up, then wait for Dominic. After that, I explore the garden, admiring the beautiful flowering bushes and the hedges that create private spaces here and there.

I've just returned to the spot where I'd set up my equipment when Dom shows up wearing his cricket kit. I've always thought the outfit professional cricketers wear are kind of sexy—pants and a polo shirt or T-shirt, plus a cap. Well, shoes too. But those don't turn me on. Dom's team always wore polo shirts that were blue with red streaks and that hugged their muscular torsos Maybe I find the cricket outfits hot because I've only ever seen men dressed that way when I was watching Dominic's team compete in matches.

He's holding a canvas bag, which he now drops on the ground. "This is your show. Command me, Chelsea."

That statement sends a tingle of excitement sweeping down my body from head to toe. *No sex today, remember? This is a photo shoot only.* "Did you bring your bat and ball?"

"Yes." He pulls them out of the bag. "Now what?"

"Stand in front of the hedge over there." While he gets in position, I pick up my camera. "Great. Stand right there."

"Aren't you going to use your tripod?"

"Not this time." I peer at him through my camera lens. "Okay, let's start with you holding your bat and ball. Try to add a little action to it, like tossing the ball or whatever you'd like."

He does what I suggested with absolutely no complaints. He's smiling too, without needing me to prod him to do that. Then he begins to adopt different poses without any cajoling, like holding his bat as if he's about to swing it or pretending to bowl.

"Haven't you always been the batsman?" I ask. "But you're pretending to throw the ball."

"Why did you ask me to bring a ball if you don't want me to do anything with it? Besides, I have served as bowler during practice matches."

"I wasn't chastising you. Keep going. I love everything you've been doing."

After a while, we move out of the garden so Dom can pose while leaning against a tree. I don't intend to ask him to take his shirt off, but he does it anyway. Once I've gotten enough shots of him and the tree, I lead him out to the makeshift pitch and ask him to pretend that he's batting.

He does that a few times, then stops. "This would be better if someone actually bowled for me."

"Thought your teammates were out of commission today."

"I can ask Hugh to do it."

"Great idea."

By the end of our session, with Hugh's help I've got more than enough pictures. In the following days, I photograph all the cricketers outdoors, including action shots. But the closer we get to the big day, the more I expect Dominic to turn anxious and grumpy again. He doesn't, though. And that's when I know one thing for sure, without any evidence to support my belief.

Dom's team will kick those youngsters' asses at Lord's.

Chapter Twenty-Three

Dominic

raining has been a grueling experience for all of us, but we've made incredible progress. I no longer feel like a mummified cricketer who was excavated from an ancient tomb. I feel at ease on the pitch—even our makeshift one here at Sommerleigh—and my teammates have grown adept at their assigned positions. Yes, I'm optimistic about our chances. More than optimistic, actually. We will do well in the charity match.

I'm standing on the pitch alone after our training session when Chelsea comes round the corner of the house and blows me a kiss from a distance. My body seems to have a mind of its own since my shoulders roll back, my chin lifts, and suddenly I know with complete certainty that it doesn't matter whether my team wins or loses. We'll be winners either way.

How many retirees get the chance to kick the arses of much younger men? As long as we don't have eleven mutual heart attacks on the field, we will have accomplished something we can all be proud of and brag about for the rest of our lives.

Chelsea disappears round the back of the house again. But she returns just as I'm leaving the lawn. And she has two more women with her.

"Good afternoon, ladies," I say as I stop beside Chelsea. "I wasn't expecting to see these two. Is this your doing?"

"Yes. We talked about your cousin Poppy a few weeks ago, so Diana and I thought we should invite her to Sommerleigh and to the big match."

"When is that?" Poppy asks.

"In three days."

Diana skims her gaze over me from top to bottom. "Training for the charity match has given you a manly glow."

I have a what? Never heard of "manly glow" before. But I graciously accept her bizarre compliment, and we all go inside to sit in the drawing room and chat. I haven't seen Poppy in ages. She's always busy with her London bookshop, and I live way out in a small village.

"How is your business going, Poppy?" I ask. "Must be a challenge to run your own bookshop."

"It is, but I love my work. Finding unusual books and first editions for my customers is very rewarding."

"But you don't have much time for dating, do you?" Diana asks. "A lovely, clever girl like you shouldn't be shut up in a bookshop day after day. When was the last time you took a day off?"

"Don't be rude," I say. "Leave Poppy alone. If she wants to date, she'll have no trouble finding someone."

"May I say something about my own life?" Poppy asks. "Or will you lot discuss that without me? I'm quite happy, by the way. Not pining for a Prince Charming to sweep me off my feet."

"Glad to hear it," I say. "Now, let's eat some of these lovely scones Kendall brought us. They go perfectly with the tea."

"I didn't mean to offend you, love," Diana tells Poppy. "I was trying to be helpful, that's all."

"Yes, I know. And I'm not upset. But finding a good man isn't as easy as everyone seems to think."

"Oh, I'm well aware of that. I had to hire a bodyguard when I had no real need for one in order to meet my perfect man." Diana reaches out to pat Poppy's knee. "If you want to get married and start a family, I have no doubts the right man will find you."

"Diana believes in fate now," Chelsea says. "And so do I. Listening to all the stories about how your friends and family found love proves that."

I roll my eyes. "It proves that our mates have gone insane with meddling in other people's lives."

Finally, our discussion moves on to other topics, and eventually, Diana and Poppy leave us.

Three days later, we head for Lord's.

Am I nervous? Only a little bit. But it's the kind of nerves every player should have right before a match, the sort that keeps us sharp and ready to go.

My parents meet us at the venue, in the luxurious private suite where they will watch the match and have the best view possible. Lord and Lady Sommerleigh, along with Rosalyn, provided the accommodations and will keep Mum and Dad company.

When Chelsea and I walk into the suite, Mum rushes up to us and pulls my girlfriend into a very boisterous hug. Then she kisses Chelsea's cheek. "It's so wonderful to see you again, love. We miss you almost as much as Dominic does whenever you go back to America."

"I missed you guys too," Chelsea says. "I'll be hanging out with everybody here in this suite, so we can watch the match together. Have you met the Parrishes before?"

"Oh, yes. But we don't get to see them as often as we'd like. Having friends and family here is a wonderful gift."

Dad, who had been loitering behind Mum, finally steps forward to hug Chelsea. "You look even more beautiful than the last time we saw you."

She kisses his cheek. "I'm so happy to you see guys."

My father gets a sly look on his face. "I saw that calendar. You are a brilliant photographer, Chelsea, though piccies of naked men aren't my cup of tea."

"I didn't expect you would swoon over it. But I'm sure you'll enjoy having a crowd of women to hang out with in this amazing suite."

Dad slaps my arm. "Glad you finally realized Chelsea is the woman for you."

"So am I." My gaze veers to Chelsea. "What did you mean about a crowd of women? There's only you, Mum, Rosalyn, and Avery."

A secretive smile makes the corners of her sealed lips curl up a touch. "You'll see."

The door opens, and Poppy rushes up to us. She hugs us both. "Won't this be a wonderful day? Dom will destroy his opponents, and tonight, we will celebrate at the gala."

Derek and Diana enter the suite next, followed swiftly by Dane and Rika Dixon. Chelsea grins and laughs when she greets them, clearly loving that we have so many mates and family members here to celebrate this day with us.

But I have a surprise for her.

When I move toward the door, Chelsea grasps my arm. "Where are you going? It's not time for you to put on your cricket kit yet."

"No, but I have a gift for you."

I pull the door open, poke my head out, and shout, "You can come in now."

Then I move aside to let our new guests inside.

Chelsea shrieks and jumps up and down. I've never seen her this excited before, but I know it's entirely because of the gift I've brought her.

Chelsea's parents have entered the suite.

Once they've both hugged their daughter, and the women have cried because they're so happy to see each other, I get a similar treatment. The Vances have always treated me like a son, but maybe soon I'll be their son-in-law. How will Chelsea feel about that? Nine years is long enough to wait.

But right now, I have a battle to wage. It's the retirees versus the youngsters.

After chatting to everyone for a bit longer, Dane and I head for the dressing room to get our kit on. As team captain, I walk out onto the field half an hour before the match is set to begin to participate in the coin toss. My team wins the right to bat first, purely by chance.

Once all the official ceremonial rubbish is done, it's time to for the battle to begin.

I take my batsman position as striker, in front of the wicket, facing the opposing team's bowler. My pulse has accelerated, but it's not fear or anxiety causing that. It's the thrill of standing on the Lord's pitch again after so many years away from the sport, and the thrill of knowing everyone I love will watch and cheer for me and my teammates. Whatever the end result might be, I will never regret having done this.

And I would never have done it without Chelsea's encouragement.

I raise my bat. The bowler launches the ball.

And I swing. The ball collides with my bat and flies across the pitch, past the bowler and the umpire and my fellow batsman, Colton Ward, sailing toward the outfield. Ward and I race toward opposite wickets and complete two runs before the ball finally drops onto the grass.

So far so good.

I glance up at the suite where Chelsea and the others are watching us. I can't make out any faces, but I know she's following every play and praying my team will win. Bolstered by the knowledge that the woman I love is watching, I bat again. This time, we don't need to run. I hit the ball so hard that it flies all the way to the boundary, giving us credit for four runs. On my next strike, I knock it past the bowler and umpire, at an angle that ensures it will land on the grass somewhere out of their reach. We make another run, and the ball lands in the grass despite one bloke's valiant attempt to grab it by leaping through the air sideways.

After four more bowls, the first over ends. A new bowler takes the field, and the match goes on in a new over. This time, Colton Ward takes up the bat, and we will both need to run like the blazes if we mean to win this match.

Chapter Twenty-Four

Chelsea

I know a T20 match lasts about three hours, but it feels like it takes forever. I'm not bored with the game. But I can't stop worrying about how Dominic will feel if his team loses, or if he makes a mistake that winds up removing him from the match. Yeah, okay, I'm being silly. Dominic knows how to handle himself on the field and how to deal with losing. He swore to me that he won't get upset if his team doesn't win. All he cares about is playing at Lord's one more time and helping to bring in more charitable donations in the process.

But I can't remember how all the weird cricket rules work, despite years of having a cricketer as my friend. So I turn to the experts—the Brits who occupy this suite with me and my parents.

"Hey, guys," I call out. "The American idiot has some questions. Who wants to try to explain cricket to me? The measly amount of information I'd already learned about it seems to have flown out of my head."

Lord Sommerleigh leans over his wife's lap, getting as close to me as he can. "I'm sure that's not true. But what would you like to know?"

"Dom told me there are six bowls per over, and twenty overs per innings, plus two innings per match."

"Correct."

"Um, how many of each of those has happened?"

Hugh chuckles. "Relax, Chelsea. All you need to know is that after the first innings, the teams will switch places. Dom's team will send in a bowler while the others take fielding positions."

"Uh-huh." I must sound confused because I am. "Never mind. I can't focus on details right now."

He gives my hand a light squeeze. "We will let you know whenever something important happens."

"Thank you. Sorry I'm being so annoying."

"You are nothing of the sort."

Hugh sits back in his seat, and I keep watching this bizarre sport. Apparently, they've just finished an innings, but instead of switching places, the teams just seem to be milling around. I guess it's break time. Why do they call it an innings, plural? It means one inning has ended. That's what they say in baseball, but cricketers just have to be different and use the plural word innings when they really should use the singular construction.

The break ends, and the second innings begins.

Derek Hahn, who has been sitting behind me, leans over the back of my seat. "There will be ten more overs, then it's...over."

He winks, then sits back in his seat.

Out on the pitch, Dane Dixon and the other umpire, who I don't know, trot back to their positions. Two players from the professional team become the batsmen, while Declan O'Hara takes over as bowler.

If there are two innings and twenty overs per innings, with six bowls per over then that means there are how many left? I do the math in my head as best I can. I think there will be ten overs of six bowls each, which adds up to sixty bowls. *Holy cow*. If I've calculated right, that sounds like a lot. I hadn't wondered about the number of bowls until after the first innings ended. Jeez, all this jargon is making my head spin.

Fortunately, our hosts had ordered food for us. Eating takes my mind off the crazy jargon and even crazier rules, allowing me to focus on keeping track of the retirees' team. The first bowler from the pro team pitches the ball—they don't call it that, but so what—and the striker aka the first batsman hits the ball. It flies so far across the field that I lose track of it. The two batsmen complete three runs before the ball whumps down in the grass at the very edge of the field.

That was impressive. These pros might beat our team.

No, they won't. Dominic and his men will find a way to trounce those upstarts. They have the advantage of experience.

The game—pardon me, match—goes on and on and on with the pro team scoring run after run. But our guys still have more than the pros do, and I clasp my hands under my chin as I sort of pray that the other team won't score more runs and win the match. This is for charity, so I shouldn't care. But I really, really do care.

I lean over Avery to ask Hugh, "I can't remember. Did our guys get out at all?"

"Yes. Colton Ward got caught out when a fielder from the opposing team managed to catch Ward's ball. He had to leave the field, and Benno Hochberg took his place."

On and on and on the game goes, while I give up trying to follow the plays and just keep my eye on Dominic. He almost catches the ball three times but misses, despite leaping up to grab for it. One of his teammates snags a ball too, but I can't tell which man that is. I can recognize Dominic strictly from the way he moves.

Well, he also has his number on the back of his shirt. I don't remember the other men's numbers.

I turn to Avery. "I've lost count. How many overs is that now?"

She looks to her husband. "This is the tenth over. Right, Hugh?"

"Yes. And it's the fifth bowl. The match is winding down, in terms of time. But those blokes are not slowing down at all." He springs forward and points at the field. "Look. Our men just bowled out the opposing team's batsman. There isn't much time left for them to score a winning run. Only one point separates the two sides."

"Dominic's team could still win?" I ask.

"It's possible."

I jump out of my seat and move closer to the railing, holding a hand above my eyes like a shield. The sun was almost blinding me.

Poppy offers me a pair of binoculars. "You won't want to miss it if Dominic's team catches the ball on the final bowl."

"Thank you."

I raise the binoculars and adjust the focus until I can see the outfield well enough to recognize the men's faces. I'll definitely see it if one of them catches the ball.

The striker for the other team hits the ball and sends it flying across the field, arching high above the heads of the other players. Hugo Carter sprints away, trying to grab the ball, but it's moving away from him too fast. Dominic is further away, better positioned to nab the thing, so he bolts across the field, raising his arm. As the ball's trajectory slowly shifts downward, he does the most amazing thing. Dominic stretches his arm out and up, launches himself several feet off the ground, and snags the ball like a freaking superhero.

And he lands on his feet, ball in hand, grinning like I've never seen him do before.

I shriek and pump my arms in the air.

The rest of his team surrounds him, whooping and cheering, while more than thirty thousand spectators more scream too.

"Get out there," Hugh hollers. "Dom will want to see you as soon as he's off the field."

"Where do I go?"

"Follow me."

Hugh hustles for the door, and I race to keep up with him as he guides down the stairs, through a long hallway, and outside. I can't help myself. I keep shrieking and clapping, jumping up and down too. Hugh watches me while grinning and laughing. Then a familiar figure sprints up to us.

"Did you see that?" Dominic says. His grin gets even bigger, despite the fact he's breathing hard from running. "We won, Chelsea. We fucking won!"

He sweeps me up in his arms and kisses me.

Chapter Twenty-Five

Dominic

The day after the most epic cricket win in the history the world, I still can't believe it really happened. All right, maybe it wasn't *that* big. But to me it is epic. A group of retired cricketers beat the youngsters. We did that, all of us together. I'd had my doubts about whether this team could pull together enough to at least not get beaten to a pulp, and I never imagined we might actually win.

My final catch shocked everyone, including me, and it even made the front pages of various newspapers. The Dom achieved one final bit of glory, and now he's happily retired for good.

Hugh and Avery invited me and Chelsea, as well as our parents, to stay at Sommerleigh for the weekend. Of course we said yes. The lawn is still decked out as a makeshift cricket ground, but I don't feel like picking up a bat. The grand match at Lord's was my swan song, and I don't feel sad about that. Chelsea suggests we go for a walk, and we wind up on the pitch. Neither of us intended to come here. But once we left the house, we found ourselves walking in this direction.

We amble onto the pitch, where the two wickets are still standing upright.

I lead us to the nearest wicket.

Chelsea slips her arm around my waist. "You look like a man with something to say."

"You know me so well." I take a moment to gather my courage, then press on. "Everything that's happened to me lately came about because of you. No one else could have inspired me more than you have and given me the strength to try for one last triumph on the field. Thank you, darling. I love you with everything I am."

"Oh Dom, I love you that much too." She swivels her head as if surveying the lawn. "Almost can't believe it's all over. What now?"

"I have some ideas. Let me explain them to you." I wrap an arm around her shoulders. "Never have I bowled a maiden over during a match, but I wouldn't mind that if I could be your slip and watch your sexy arse."

"Benno tried a 'maiden over' joke too. Yours is much hotter, though. I think it's your voice that nails it."

"I'd love to bowl straight into your wicket."

"Damn, I can't believe how horny you're making me with all this goofy cricket jargon. Don't stop."

"Hmm." I nuzzle her ear. "May I plumb your middle stump?"

"Not out here. Let's go into the garden."

"Should I bring a ball so you can show me your cherry?"

"Oh God, yes."

I guide her away from the lawn and deep inside the garden. Its many paths and the trees that arch over them provide perfect cover for a daytime shag. We choose a spot surrounded by a trio of large, flowering bushes backed by an apple tree, the branches of which overhang the bushes. I don't even need to tell Chelsea to undress. She does that as soon as we reach our little hideaway, and I follow her lead. Before we get started, I retrieve a condom from my trouser pocket, then roll it onto my cock.

Chelsea lies down, spreading her legs for me.

I drink in the beauty of her body. "Feel free to bowl my bodyline, darling. I can handle it."

"No idea what that means, but hearing you speak those words makes me even wetter."

I lie down beside her. The grass is green, soft, and fragrant as if it's been recently mowed. "You are the captain. That means climb on top of me and go at it, love."

"Please don't call me skipper. That's not sexy." She climbs astride me and slowly lowers herself onto my length. "Touch me, Dom, please."

I grasp her hips, then slide my hands up to her chest, grazing the sides of her breasts with my fingertips. When I stretch my thumbs out to rub her nipples, her eyes fall partway closed and her tongue peeks out between her open lips. She begins to move, rocking gently.

"You are The Dom," she murmurs. "And I love the way you feel inside me. Bowl me over or maiden my stump or whatever, I don't care."

I might chuckle if she weren't riding me in such an erotic way. Can't think of any more filthy things to whisper to her. But words do tumble out of me. "I want to spend the rest of my life with you, Chelsea. Marry me."

She stares at me wide-eyed. "What?"

"Uh, I think I asked you to marry me."

"You think?" Somehow, she manages to keep fucking me even while she gapes at me.

"I'm sure. Marry me. As soon as possible."

She suddenly goes wild, pounding her body onto my cock hard and fast, gasping and shouting my name while her cries echo off the house a hundred yards away. I don't even have time to rub her clit. She comes without warning, and as her body milks me fiercely, I come too with a hoarse bellow.

Chelsea slides off me but remains sitting up. "Ask me again, right now."

I push up onto my elbows and meet her gaze. "Will you marry, Chelsea?"

She grins. "Yes."

How do we celebrate? By shagging, of course.

Later, we agree to get married as soon as possible. When we share the news with our parents, they're thrilled. Chelsea's mum and dad want to move to England to be closer to their daughter and soon-to-be son-in-law. Her father is recently retired, and her mother has run an at-home handicraft business over the internet for years. That means all we need to do is find them a proper home. In the meantime, they will stay at my house along with Chelsea.

That night, we all attend the charity gala. The venue is enormous and splendidly decorated. I can't believe how many people are here, including many of our mates. The professional cricketers that my team had played against approach us to share their congratulations, and after that, we chat to each other for a while. The gala includes music and dancing too, and Chelsea and I take to the floor several times.

But one of the party guests surprises us both.

A man in a tuxedo who seems rather familiar comes up to us as we finish our last dance. "Good evening, Mr. Rigby. Good evening, Miss Vance."

I stare at him for several seconds before I recognize him. "Kendall?"

"Yes, sir, it's me. Lord and Lady Sommerleigh insisted I come to the gala ball. They've also invited me to the Halloween do they and all their mates are planning." Kendall leans forward a touch and lowers his voice to a whisper. "They say it will be the incredible Halloween bash ever."

"Maybe you'll meet a girl there. If you don't already have one."

"No, sir, I don't."

"Well, go dance with someone. Right now."

He grins and hurries away, apparently to fulfill my command.

I lead Chelsea back to our table, which we share with several of our mates, and we sit down to take a break from the revelry.

Chelsea crosses her legs and eyes me with a devious smile. "Maybe we could help Kendall find a girlfriend. Halloween isn't that far away, so…"

"No meddling."

She slants toward me, laying a hand on my thigh. "Come on. We have to help Kendall. He works hard, and he's so sweet. Plus, he's damn hot in a tux." She slants even closer until her lips graze my cheek. "I want to do this. Don't you want to make me happy?"

Chelsea slides her hand up to my groin.

"Yes, all right, you win." I peel her hand away from my cock. "Let's meddle."

Want more of Kendall?
Experience his story in *One Hot Bash* (Hot Brits, Book Ten).

Love the

Hot Brits

series?

Visit

AnnaDurand.com

to subscribe to her newsletter

for updates on forthcoming books in this series

&

to receive free gifts for signing up!

Anna Durand is a bestselling, multi-award-winning author of contemporary and paranormal romance. Her books have earned bestseller status on every major retailer and wonderful reviews from readers around the world. But that's the boring spiel. Here are the really cool things you want to know about Anna!

Born on Lackland Air Force Base in Texas, Anna grew up moving here, there, and everywhere thanks to her dad's job as an instructor pilot. She's lived in Texas (twice), Mississippi, California (twice), Michigan (twice), and Alaska—and now Ohio.

As for her writing, Anna has always made up stories in her head, but she didn't write them down until her teen years. Those first awful books went into the trash can a few years later, though she learned a lot from those stories. Eventually, she would pen her first romance novel, the paranormal romance *Willpower*, and she's never looked back since.

Want even more details about Anna? Get access to her extended bio when you subscribe to her newsletter and download the free bonus ebook, *Hot Scots Confidential*. You'll also get hot deleted scenes, character interviews, fun facts, and more! Plus you'll receive the short story *Tempted by a Kiss* and mutliple bonus chapters in both ebook and audiobook formats.

Visit AnnaDurand.com to sign up.